MW01257647

Into the Ruins

Issue 7
Fall 2017

Cover art copyright © 2017 by W. Jack Savage

Cover and interior design copyright © 2017 by Joel Caris

Published November 2017 by Figuration Press
Portland, Oregon

Into the Ruins is a project and publication of Figuration Press,
a small publication house focused on alternate visions of the future
and alternate ways of understanding the world,
particularly in ecological contexts.

intotheruins.com

figurationpress.com

ISBN 13: 978-0-9978656-5-3
ISBN 10: 0-9978656-5-2

Editor's Note:
Surrounded by damp, hanging laundry.
Letting evaporation do its thing.

Comments and feedback always welcome at editor@intotheruins.com
Comments for authors will be forwarded.

Issue 7
Fall 2017

TABLE OF CONTENTS

PREAMBLE

THAT COMMON BEGINNING

BY JOEL CARIS

I REMEMBER WATCHING MY WIFE CHOP VEGETABLES. Such a small thing: the familiar preparations of a meal, that common beginning. Watching her work, I marveled at the changes we had already lived. The soft evolution of her cooking throughout our two-and-a-half years together, as well as the evolution of my own; the ways we had grown so familiar with each other even as we both face decades yet of learning; the slow knitting together of our lives necessary to make something whole out of halves created in separation.

On our first date, I gifted her a dozen eggs originally marked for friends. I brought them into the city with me from my chickens out on the coast. There is, as I suspect many of you reading this know, a marked difference between a dozen eggs from a backyard coop filled with chickens who know a life of truly free roaming against those purchased at the supermarket. That sharing of good food—not a gift rooted in any particular monetary value, but in taste and experience, in an indirect connection to the landscape from which I came to see her—was an appropriate way to begin our relationship. In all the time following, it has been one rooted in good food, over and over again, a shared connection around which so many of our memories and bonds have formed.

In those early, heady days, Kate established this pattern of connection and exploration with that dozen gifted eggs. She sent me nightly emails with pictures of them crafted into meals for herself: fried and placed atop a few spears of asparagus one day, and a bowl of cooked vegetables on another; whipped and folded into a mushroom omelette; baked into a Midwest-inspired chicken casserole; and transformed into a decadent flourless chocolate cake in anticipation of our second date. Separated by geography but bound by food, we used our meals as part of our initial explorations of each other, a conversational courtship conducted by email during the weekdays and punctuated by weekend visits both at the coast and in the city. We talked not just of food, but our day-to-day lives, our backgrounds, our understandings of the world. Good food always seemed to linger as a touchstone, though, finding its way into so many subjects and consistently tying us together, threading through the way each of us came to understand the other.

The meals Kate made for us and for herself—sometimes simple, sometimes complex, but always delicious and impressive in the artistry in which she created them—helped me to better understand her. And in our conversations about them, they revealed her even more. She told me about the simple, favorite dishes she would make for herself. In time, she made them for me as well, but usually a version that featured some greater complexity, a heightened effort. It was an unnecessary gift, but each time an appreciated one. Kate took my passion, love for, and access to well-grown, well-raised food and coupled it with a mastery of use, bringing it to flower in dishes I never would have imagined or been able to design myself. That coupling has always proved potent and feels, to this day, like the forward face of our relationship: one of the easier ways to see the connection that holds us together day in and day out, even if it doesn't begin to speak to the entirety of that connection. It's a way of complementing each other that resonates—at least with me, and I suspect with others, as well.

That food may feature so prominently in our relationship is, to me, both surprising and not. On the one hand, there were moments in my childhood and adolescence when I literally thought life would be simpler and better if I did not have to worry about eating. It seemed an imposition, a complication I would rather not have to navigate. On the other hand, food has held varying kinds of importance to me for the majority of my life, and its presence and influence has only grown as I have aged.

I came to farming, in some ways, because I did not know what else to do. I had finished a late stint of college to complete my Bachelor's degree after two years spent in AmeriCorps, engaged in environmental restoration work. My degree was nothing that would guarantee me work—if such a thing even exists in the world of degrees anymore—and my halfhearted search for a job had proved, at that point, unfruitful. I did not know what I wanted to do, other than the thing I had wanted to do much of my life but never put the necessary work into accomplishing: becoming a successful writer. With that path offering no immediate income, I hardly thought of it. Instead, I turned to a subject I had been reading and learning about: local food systems.

The idea of working for a small-scale farm had flirted around the edge of my consciousness, thanks to a few friends from AmeriCorps who had interned on farms themselves, or otherwise found some way into local food systems work. At the time, I didn't know if it would work for me. I had not grown up a person involved in physical labor, nor particularly interested in it. My suburban childhood had included summertime efforts in my father's garden, true, and I enjoyed the outside world within the context of camping, hiking, exploring, and other low-intensity, noncompetitive activities, but I also enjoyed spending time within my own head. I enjoyed the comforts and conveniences of the human-built world. I enjoyed media and distraction—even technological gadgets, to a certain degree. The people I met in AmeriCorps and the different kinds of culture it exposed me to had started the process of breaking me free from these interests and pursuits and nudging me toward a different life—one more sustainable, less intensive, less prone to distraction, and skeptical of many of the trappings of the modern world and American culture in particular. I wanted meaningful work and to improve the world, and I wanted to continue to explore the growing skepticism within myself about the ways in which we so commonly conduct business in this country.

And so I began to search for a farm. Having made the decision in June, my timing was poor, but the islands scattered across the Puget Sound offered me a few opportunities for a seasonal farm internship, and I soon found myself on Whidbey Island, diving into full time physical labor and beginning the process of learning how to grow food.

Over the course of that summer, the natural world opened up around me. Or, if I'm to be precise, I opened to it. While challenging in a number of ways, growing food proved to be incredibly rewarding work, and the experience of working on a farm accelerated many of the changes that had started with my time in AmeriCorps. As I grew stronger and more fit, lost weight, and increased my stamina, the joys of physical work became more and more apparent to me. The knock on effects of working out in the field revealed themselves: better and more satisfying sleep at regular times, increased energy, better clarity of thought, and improved self-confidence. I felt more competent than at most any other time of my life. I worked and read, ate and drank, wrote letters, socialized. I did not spend much time staring at screens. The trailer I lived in received no wifi and I did not have a smart phone. I grew less distracted.

As I learned to follow the seasonal cycles of the food I was helping to grow, I also became fully aware of the seasonal cycles in the natural world around me for the first time. I caught the very first turnings of fall: the first crisp chills in the nighttime air, the first leaves changing color, the dying back of certain plants, all those early signs that can so easily be missed. I caught them because I was outside daily; I was there. In my previous life, it seemed I noticed the season had changed only once it gripped the outer world fully, forcing me to notice it during my brief trips between my car and whatever destination I had arrived at. That first summer farming, being outside every day for much of the day, I saw the very first flirtations, the beginning of the courtship. I watched the seasons as they revealed themselves, and that experience was a revelation for me, as well.

The details of that time farming abound: the way Charlie, a brilliant Anatolian Shepherd who was the farm dog, would wake me up early in the morning, barking at the bald eagles perched in the firs towering next to the Airstream trailer that served as my home; the way my clothes hung strange on me after a summer of extreme weight loss, spurred by far more physical labor than I had ever engaged in before coupled with a heavily vegetarian diet much lighter than any I had eaten before; how I came to know and love that land and find a new kind of peace by working on it; evening ferry rides back from Port Townsend, the nearest town with some kind of social scene, where I would go when I needed to spend an evening having a beer, watching a movie, and being around other people; the melancholy loneliness that sometimes took hold of me, far away from home, from family and friends, limited in the number of people I interacted with and yearning for certain connections I could not find there.

It may be that in my recounting of the time, it comes across as purely good. It was not that. It was intensely challenging, at times very lonely, isolating, and there were times I was filled with doubt. And yet, it was also intensely rewarding, full of camaraderie with my farm companions, intense with joy and connection, and imbued me with a confidence the likes of which I had yet to experience. Thinking back on those months, they're wrapped with an intensity of emotion and revelation. I became a different person there. I reset my life. And I discovered a kind of world that I had not known before, but that once discovered, I could not turn my back on. By the end of that season, I thought myself a farmer. I did not know if I always would be, but I did not believe I could erase the experience and what it had created of me from my life. In some way, going forward, I would always be a farmer.

I am not a farmer these days. But food is still there; it is always there. I have a small, if unimpressive garden in my back yard, withering away now in the fall months. I have friends who farm. Sometimes I walk their field and talk with them, picking their brains about varieties and strategies, disease and pests, yields and vigor, the flavor of what they grow. I can and preserve. I cook. Sometimes I open a seed catalog and fall into it, a past world raging around me.

I am a husband now, and that is as new to me as farming was back in the summer of 2009. Each day it reveals itself a bit more to me, and I sometimes marvel at what I may know in ten years time, twenty years, more. I expect at that point I will still be married, but one can never know. Regardless, though, I will always be a husband as I will always be a farmer. I know that without hesitation. It is something already now entering my blood, settling deep in my mind, changing me irrevocably. The world can now never go back to what it was before; Kate and our relationship has changed me as markedly as when I came to know and live and breathe that land on Whidbey Island, bringing forth food from it.

There is a transformation inherent in both that echoes in me, and there are ways that it seems one led to the other. If I had not made the decision to farm some eight-and-a-half years ago, I don't imagine I ever would have met Kate, let alone married her. Granted, such a claim could be made with some degree of confidence in regards to many random actions I've taken over the years. So many decisions define and refine a path that just one altered can easily veer one off an important and precise future point along that path. But it's more than just that happenstance: I do think food anchored us in our relationship. Farming led to Kate; I see no other way to understand it. And that work brought me to be the person she fell in love with, and who fell in love with her.

It's a matter of depth, of completion. Farming made me into someone more connected with the natural world, more thoughtful about my actions, and more determined to lead a life of intention rather than one of drifting. It both refined and defined me, and that refinement and definition still echoes strongly today. I think back on my life before farming and I am unsure of who I would be today if not for that divergence. I'm not sure I would want to know. I can hardly imagine that person.

Yet I also fear for that person—or would, if that person were to exist. The thing about farming is that it helped bring me in line with the future I expect to see. It taught me how to grow food, yes, but it also taught me how to live with less. It taught me about simplicity and connection, about how good a life one can lead with little money but with good work, good health, good food, and good friends. Provide those four elements and it is shocking how little else you need. Food, shelter, protection, a sense of worth built through good work, a healthy body, a place to belong, and people to bring you joy and companionship; give me those and I can live through perhaps any future. In fact, the great fear I have for any future of mine is losing one or more of those elements. It is not in the loss of excess material goods, wealth, or a wide range of comforts and conveniences; it's in the loss of good meals, excellent conversation, meaningful work, very basic comfort and shelter, and the companionship of someone I love and trust and can give myself to.

Here, too, I see the connection between farming and being a husband. Both of these promise themselves sustainable in an uncertain future. In a time of turmoil and disruption, growing food is work that can sustain at all levels: providing food, meaning, and worth. Similarly, being a good husband is work that also can sustain in times no matter how hard: providing companionship and comfort for both myself and my wife, the basis of both a home and a household economy to sustain ourselves, and a joy found in each other that hardship cannot take away unless we allow it to. In my experience, love well fought for and enjoyed is as rewarding as good work accomplished. Both of them provide the basis for some of the most elemental pleasure we can experience.

In both becoming a farmer and becoming a husband, I have found meaning. I've discovered the joys of feeding people and I've discovered the joys of building a life together with another person. In both instances, the pursuit of something more meaningful has allowed me to grow into a better person, even if in fits and starts. And it has allowed me to shed elements of my living that, looking back, were pointless and even demeaning. I have far less time now for useless distractions and shallow entertainments. That does not mean I have shed them completely, but as the far more meaningful tasks and needs spread themselves out in front of me, I find myself less interested in devoting time to the unmeaningful ones. There is a life better lived waiting for me.

These are the kinds of changes, even if made in fits and starts, that I believe help to prepare us for what may be a hard future. There will always be good work to do. There will always be important people to build meaningful lives with. There will always be tasks at hand needed to make the world that slightest bit better—and they will become ever more important as we face the consequences of our collective actions. Growing food and growing a relationship with someone I love deeply both help better prepare me for the future we face. And in finding pleasure in those experiences, I help secure pleasures that are far more likely to remain with me while other, far more transitory ones are stripped away by necessity. Perhaps I will not have screens at some point in the future. That won't much matter to me if I have good work, good meals, and someone I love to share them with.

Yesterday I visited my ragged, dying garden. As the rain and cold set in, most of the plants began to die back, and new growth dramatically slowed as the hours of available sunlight dwindled. I have therefore paid little attention to the garden of late, instead transitioning fully to eating from our CSA share and what we supplement it with from the farmers market. Yet, peering into the foliage of one of my powdery mildew-covered zucchini plants, I discovered two small but substantial zucchinis, looking in fine health and high spirits, apparently waiting for the opportunity to become part of a meal. Pleased, I broke them off the plants stalks, brought them into our kitchen, and showed Kate this small harvest. Then this morning, we ate a zucchini and shallot scramble for breakfast.

It was just one small moment in what I hope will be a lifetime of growing food and eating it, those ritual actions providing the background rhythms of a lifelong marriage. I don't know what the broader world will bring us in that time; what joys and pleasures, what hardships and upheavals, what turmoil, what calm, what successes and failures, trials and tribulations. I hope it will be less hard than I fear—that my cynicism will prove unfounded, as it sometimes is. But even if it isn't, food will always be there, and it will always be part of what binds me to Kate. Kate, too—if I am lucky, if she is patient—will always be there, and we will always be making a life together, finding a great deal of pleasure in it even as we find the occasional challenges, as well.

It's a comfort to me: I will always be a farmer and I will always be a husband. In that sustenance and companionship, in the good work inherent and necessary in both, I believe Kate and I will always be able to make something beautiful out of this world. And as likely as not, it will begin with one of us chopping vegetables: that common beginning, the basis of everything.

— Portland, Oregon
November 13, 2017

Don't miss Catherine McGuire's new novel, *Lifeline*, now available in print and e-book formats via Founders House Publishing!

Learn more and purchase a copy for yourself at http://www.foundershousepublishing.com/2017/03/lifeline-novel.html

Into the Ruins is published quarterly by Figuration Press. We publish deindustrial science fiction that explores a future defined by natural limits, energy and resource depletion, industrial decline, climate change, and other consequences stemming from the reckless and shortsighted exploitation of our planet, as well as the ways that humans will adapt, survive, live, die, and thrive within this future.

One year, four issue subscriptions to *Into the Ruins* are $39. You can subscribe by visiting intotheruins.com/subscribe or by mailing a check made out to Figuration Press to:

Figuration Press / 3515 SE Clinton Street / Portland, OR 97202

To submit your work for publication, please visit intotheruins.com/submissions or email submissions@intotheruins.com.

All issues of *Into the Ruins* are printed on paper, first and foremost. Electronic versions will be made available as high quality PDF downloads. Please visit our website for more information. The opinions expressed by the authors do not necessarily reflect the opinions of Figuration Press or *Into the Ruins*. Except those expressed by Joel Caris, since this is a sole proprietorship. That said, all opinions are subject to (and commonly do) change, for despite the Editor's occasional actions suggesting the contrary, it turns out he does not know everything and the world often still surprises him.

EDITOR-IN-CHIEF
JOEL CARIS

ASSOCIATE EDITOR
SHANE WILSON

DESIGNER
JOEL CARIS

WITH THANKS TO
SHANE WILSON
JOHN MICHAEL GREER
OUR SUBSCRIBERS

SPECIAL THANKS TO
KATE O'NEILL

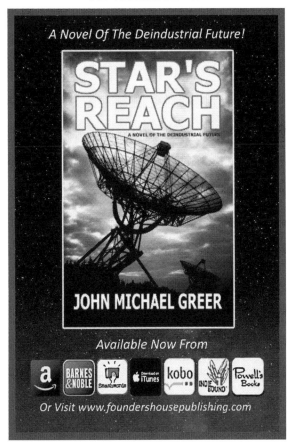

CONTRIBUTORS

JOEL CARIS is a gardener and homesteader, occasional farmer, passionate advocate for local and community food systems, sporadic writer, voracious reader, sometimes prone to distraction and too attendant to detail, a little bit crazy, a cynical optimist, and both deeply empathetic toward and frustrated with humanity. He is your friendly local editor and publisher. As a reader of this journal and perhaps other writings of his, he hopes you don't too easily tire of his voice and perspective. He lives in Oregon with his all-too-amazing wife.

W. JACK SAVAGE is a retired broadcaster and educator. He is the author of seven books, including *Imagination: The Art of W. Jack Savage* (wjacksavage.com). To date, more than fifty of Jack's short stories and over seven hundred of his paintings and drawings have been published worldwide. Jack and his wife Kathy live in Monrovia, California. Jack is, as usual, responsible for this issue's cover art.

DAMIAN MACRAE spent his formative years on a dairy farm watching Star Trek and reading dusty paperbacks from the likes of King, Vance and Herbert. Fleeing the family farm weeks after completing high school he has worked various IT jobs across Australia before moving to Hobart, Tasmania to study surveying where he learned to brew beer, stew rabbit and keep chooks. After two years working underground and a volunteer assignment in Laos he now resides in Christchurch, New Zealand with his partner. In between working and writing he dreams of owning a small farm, perhaps with some chooks. Occasionally, he threatens to build a wooden sail-boat.

AL SEVCIK'S fiction has recently appeared in *After Oil: Volume 3*, the *Merigan Tales* anthology, and *Into the Ruins*. After graduation from Hilo High in Hawaii, he earned degrees in technology and business and spent two years in the Air Force. Al and his wife live in Tampa, Florida.

G.KAY BISHOP began writing as a child poet: free and assured, joyful and solemn, forever lauding the incandescence of nature or gleefully roasting bloody gobbets of human cruelty, spitted on sharpened sticks of satire, turned nice and slow over the coals of divine wrath. This has not changed much over time. Age is no barrier to an artist's eternal immaturity.

N.B.: Poetry has its occupational hazards. When one has the inveterate habit of deep listening for the apt word, stories sometimes come along and roughly demand to be written. Never argue with the Muses if you know what's good for ya. They may not break your knees, but they can do a real number on ya. If you find yourself browsing the Shorter Oxford, fondling strange adjectives, slipping obscure nouns into other people's coffee breaks, beware. You may be suppressing an urgent flair for fiction.

DANIEL STRIDE has a lifelong love of literature in general and speculative fiction in particular. He writes both short stories and poetry; his first novel, Wise Phuul, was published in November 2016 by a small UK press. He lives in Dunedin, New Zealand, and he may be found blogging at phuulishfellow.wordpress.com

GUSTAVO BONDONI is an Argentine writer with over a hundred stories published in fourteen countries, in seven languages, and is a winner in the National Space Society's "Return to Luna" Contest and the Marooned Award for Flash Fiction (2008). His fiction has appeared in the Texas STAAR English Test cycle, *The Rose & Thorn*, *Albedo One*, *The Best of Every Day Fiction* and many others. His latest books are two science fiction novels: *Outside* (2017) and *Siege* (2016). He has also recently published an ebook novella entitled *Branch*. His previously published short fiction is collected in *Tenth Orbit and Other Faraway Places* (2010) and *Virtuoso and Other Stories* (2011, Dark Quest Books). *The Curse of El Bastardo* (2010) is a short fantasy novel. His website is at www.gustavobondoni.com.

LETTERS TO THE EDITOR

Dear Editor,

As I attempt, in my own muddling-through sort of way, to navigate the terrain of contraction, I find myself confronting deep-seated assumptions about myself and my role in this world—assumptions that are not necessarily true, despite their well-rooted nature. Addressing these assumptions where needed and altering my self-perceptions as required constitute no small challenge. This inner alchemy is not for the faint of heart and I have to admit that I did not have a firm grasp of the extent of challenge when I first set foot on the journey. Yet, here I am.

These changes range from the spiritually-challenging to the out-and-out surprising (not that these are mutually exclusive!)—a good example of the former being my need to watch the present political scene with equanimity and allow the system to come apart, accepting that the nature of decline and the social/economic/psychological forces at play almost guarantee that our collective choices will continue to take us along the well-worn paths of previous empires and civilizations. One concept that helps me frame the situation is the idea of Isaac Asimov's discipline of "psycho-history" from his Foundation novels.

Thinking of the forces at play in our world as psycho-historical vectors somehow makes the drama of our decline a bit more palatable.

The more surprising aspect of these changes has rather snuck up on me, as surprises are wont to do. I've been working my plots in the community garden for four seasons now and I have to admit that I feel great joy when my hands are buried in the soil of my beds or when I'm prepping the fruits of that labor in my kitchen. My wife has commented on how my energy is completely different when I am in the integrated-with-the-earth zone rather than my mind being embroiled with the state of the world. Not that long ago, she looked at me and said, "You know, you're actually a pretty good cook." Needless to say, this is has not been a prime component of my self-image up to this point.

But between my work in the community garden and a few other experiences I've had recently, I've come to realize that I am being called to the soil. And so I have put together a nine-(and a half)-year plan to transform myself from spreadsheet-wielding office fauna to muckboot-wearing small-scale agriculturalist. (I am nothing if not a planner.) Interestingly, the timeframe I am looking at is very similar to that of my grandfather when he began to farm. Of course, our backgrounds could not be more different—he grew up in the 1920s and 30s in a farming community in western Missouri with a career as a mechanic, whereas I've grown up in the 'burbs up and down the eastern seaboard as the son of a career naval officer with a career as a math geek. But I remember the farm I used to visit as a child and, while I will be nowhere near the same scale of operation, I believe that this is the direction I am meant to go. Five, perhaps ten acres in or (more likely) around the small city where I live presently would be ideal. We'll see what happens. I have a ways to go yet!

Finally, my groundedness (to follow on to your question from the previous issue) comes from the earth and her fruits. One of the small things that I do, particularly this time of year when the harvest from the garden is really coming in, is to set up my tablet in the kitchen and play compilations of epic battle music on YouTube as I clean and cut and prep. It gives me a sense of grandness in small things. Epic bean-shelling! Heroic slicing of cabbage! Mighty scrubbing of potatoes! Perhaps odd, but it works.

David England
Two Rivers, Wisconsin

Dear Editor,

I would like to let our honorable G.Kay Bishop know that her agenda against classical de-pluralization are [*sic*] honorably defended, but the ship has long since sailed. There are [*sic*] many [*sic*] interesting trivia about words with unsuspected plural origins, but ultimately the way hoi polloi talk [*sic*] is the way the language goes, and there's no stopping it. I think propaganda that insist [*sic*] that everyone needs to know their Latin and Greek declensions are [*sic*] unnecessary. But then, perhaps I'm just a *sic* person.

Chuck Masterson
Minneapolis, Minnesota

Editor's Note: I recently asked in a blog post on this magazine's website what parts of their lives did readers not expect to lose in the hardship of the coming years. In other words, what elements of their current lives did they believe were sustainable in the long run, and in what ways did those parts of their lives bring them pleasure and sustenance? On the following pagers are some of the responses I received.

LETTERS

Dear Editor,

There is very little in my home I wouldn't consider expendable. For instance, for many years I had no bed and slept on a mattress on the floor; I mostly didn't have a kitchen and mostly didn't use it even when I had one, resorting to what I call floor storage and makeshift food preparation; I never had and don't want a sofa, etc, etc. This may be whimsical of me but the only domestic implement I consider non-negotiable is a private wash machine: I left the US, where I spent nearly a decade, partly because renters there aren't allowed to have their own wash machine and having to use the communal one drove me nuts. As for hand washing, I've done that for a couple of years total, on and off, and my heart goes out to the women who were tasked with it in the past: it is the most dreadful chore. Thus I am keenly interested in technologies that bridge the gap between hand washing and present-day push-button wonders, which require electricity and complex manufacturing chains.

Other than that I can't imagine a life without books but publishing is such an old and hardy technology that surely it is not at risk of being lost. And I also pray we can retain as much as possible of the medical advances of the last century, especially antibiotics and antifungals, the former already under threat for other reasons.

Lastly, you didn't ask but I can't resist mentioning that conversely I wish we do lose all the tools of surveillance and delation that make modernity such a friend to the police state. And not being rendered destitute by robots and AIs would be nice, too. If that means losing the entire IT sector and the internet, so be it, and I am saying that as a software developer.

Olivier Lefevre
Berlin, Germany

Dear Editor,

There are a lot of broad concepts that will persist, but will still change drastically. We're talking about the end of industrial civilization, and all that brings. And as 90% of our lives are based on the things that industrial civilization provides, we're bound to see drastic changes. To know what will persist we have to look at the core, the root, of things. Culture and cars and shopping centers are transitory and will disintegrate. Relationships and teamwork and community will persist, though in very different forms. Humans are dichotomous creatures, capable of the most sublime and uplifting acts as well as the most heinous and selfish. As things collapse, I predict we'll see more and more of those two extremes. Less people will be able to be solitary, insulated, or dismissive when they and their communities are hit hard by what's coming.

David Casey
Winston Salem, North Carolina

Dear Readers,

I do not expect to lose the dead, dropped leaves of fall. I do not expect to lose the popping crackle of fire, and I do wonder if it will one day again be what keeps me warm. I do not expect to lose evaporation: the simplest kind of drying, with no mechanized intermediary necessary. I do not expect to lose the soil in which I may plant a garden, or a tree, or some other life to bloom into the world and nourish me one way or another. *Some* of the soil, yes—far too much—but not all of it.

I do not expect to lose the surroundings of other life: the squirrels in the yard, the stalking cats of the neighborhood, and the dutiful dogs walking along with their owners; the cows out on the coast, the chickens cooped everywhere, the milking goats and their young, ricocheting off the walls of barns; the birds and birds and birds, everywhere, flitting, hopping, brilliant and quick and both stealthy and loud, so many of them; the hunting, sorting raccoons; the uncountable microorganisms, unseen, anchoring all our lives.

I do not expect to lose good food and good meals. If I have to grow it myself, I will. If I have to trade for it, I will. If I have to weed, I will weed. If I have to turn the soil, consider it done. If I must save seed, I look forward to it. If my body must be sore, consider it forewarned: you will ache. Give me a task and I will help you bring forth food. In a small way, I ask about it every day.

I do not expect to lose love. It does not require oil or coal, flows of electricity, convenience or wealth, or imperial powers. It requires only patience, generosity, and care. Sometimes that is hard, but all futures provide the opportunity.

I do not expect to lose the ability to tell stories. In the end, they require only a keen mind and dedicated observation, perhaps an understanding of one's audience, and a certain curiosity. Stories are everywhere, waiting to be uncovered: in the world surrounding us, hidden deep in our minds, in the livelihoods discovered at every turn, human or otherwise. They can be spoken. They can be written on the most ragged paper. They can be even imagined and then forgotten, a momentary delight for one. There are new stories created every day, and as the world changes around us, so too will the stories. They will by necessity. And in that telling, they may prove not just free of whatever constraints we find in the coming years, but profitable of those constraints. They may yet keep us from losing so much more.

I do not expect to lose my curiosity. I will always wonder what is to happen next in this world, and I am so happy I still get to find out. I suppose one day I no longer will, and at that point I must leave the curiosity to the next generations. I will be leaving the world, too, and I apologize already that it will not be what it once was, just as it has not been for me what it once was. But even today, and no doubt tomorrow, I consider it a revelation. Whatever we lose, the world will still be there, compelling and full of life, even if we extinguish too much of it in our hubris.

With luck, one day, that is something we *will* lose. I hope then we can turn toward a true conservation and speak then not of what we may or may not lose, but in what we might bring back.

Joel Caris
Portland, Oregon

Into the Ruins welcomes letters to the editor from our readers. We encourage thoughtful commentary on the contents of this issue, the themes of the magazine, and humanity's collective future. Readers may email their letters to editor@intotheruins.com or mail them to:

Figuration Press
3515 SE Clinton Street
Portland, OR 97202

Please include your full name, city and state, and an email or phone number. Only your name and location will be printed with any accepted letter.

DISCOVER THE FIRST YEAR OF INTO THE RUINS

STORIES

ANCHORED DOWN IN ANCHORAGE

BY GUSTAVO BONDONI

PHIL CRUMPLED THE PRINTOUT. It was from his boss, reminding him that his six months of immersion were nearly up, and that he would have to file the story today or it wouldn't make the *Times*' Great New Cities special edition—and that would make everyone at the paper extremely unhappy. Did he even have a draft they could see?

The draft, forty pages of copy and the photos he recommended paper-clipped to it sat on the desk beside him. Over the past three weeks, he'd almost sent it out more times than he could count. It would have meant his Pulitzer, after all.

But he hadn't. And now he knew he wouldn't. So no prizes would be forthcoming, but at least he's chosen the lesser betrayal.

He walked out of the hotel, knowing he wouldn't be back. He hadn't actually been living there for weeks, anyway, but since the *Times* was footing the bill, he still used it as a base of operations and makeshift office.

"The New Río" was the title he'd envisioned; an article drawing parallels between social and physical characteristics of the Brazilian city of seventy-five years ago and the American city of today. But, brilliant as the concept was, it would never see the light of day. He couldn't do that to Anchorage, couldn't do it to Soledad.

He headed up the hill, sweating in the unseasonal pre-monsoon heat which presaged a night of rain. He was late, but knew he'd still get there before her.

It was hard to believe that he'd already been there six months. Where had the time gone?

The Alaskan Airlines seaplane that had brought Phil in from Seattle landed on the water just a few hundred yards beyond the submerged buildings. The old airport was, like most of the old commercial sector, under five feet of water. Anchorage hadn't had enough money or political clout to get dykes built in time—the city had been too far down on the Army Engineer's priority list—so the population had migrated to the hills.

Phil descended from the plane and boarded a large motorboat with glass-sided walls and roof. The uneventful trip to the pier allowed him to get his first glimpse of Anchorage. He'd already seen thousands of photos of the semi-submerged office buildings, so his attention was drawn to other things—the numbers of airplanes moored to the piers, to buoys or simply anchored in the sea, the fishing fleet behind him, plying the surprisingly calm sea in an attempt to get a few final harvests in before the acidification process made fishing a thing of the past.

Most of all, he was surprised at the temperature. It was very early spring, and he really hadn't known what to expect—he'd half-expected it to be as warm as summer, but then he'd also half-expected to freeze. The reality was cold, but not too cold. Good, that would be the first data point for the article.

On leaving the boat, he was accosted by a flock of rickshaw drivers, a product of the migration from the lower forty-eight, and from at least three or four south Pacific islands that no longer existed—relics of the days when the government thought that populating Alaska was something that would have to be done through opportunistic treaties.

Phil selected a smiling, dark-haired youth at random and let him load the large suitcase onto the long poles—notched to keep baggage in place—and took a seat in the rear.

"Where to, sir?" the kid asked. Southern accent, but not too extreme—maybe Kentucky. Definitely not from Vanuatu, then.

"The Hilton. But if you want to make a few extra bucks, I'd like a tour of the city."

"Can we drop off the suitcase first?"

Phil smiled. An Indian driver would carry an elephant on his poles all over Kolkota for a few rupees. But this wasn't India, this was America. Overcrowded, dirty, under-policed, but America. A real life twenty-first century boom town.

"Okay," he replied.

They checked him into the New Anchorage Hilton—the old one, though still standing, had been deemed structurally unsafe when the water reached a couple of feet. Anyway, guests had been avoiding the water-logged hotel for years. The company had accepted its losses and built from scratch far enough up a hill that they wouldn't have that particular problem again for a few hundred years.

The city had the raw, unsafe feel of frontier towns everywhere. Phil wasn't particularly worried. His time with the Marines in the euphemistically named "Police Action" had put him in worse cesspools than this one on a regular basis—and back then, any time the Chinese army wasn't shooting at them had been considered R&R.

But it still felt weird to be riding a rickshaw over a muddy dirt street winding its way through a shantytown of wood and corrugated houses on American soil. There were plenty of migrant slums in the lower forty-eight, but nothing like this.

"So, who's the big dope dealer in town?" Phil asked the kid.

"I have no idea."

Yeah, right. "I can pay for the information."

"Money ain't no good to me if I'm feeding the fish, mister. You some kinda cop?"

"A reporter. I'm doing a story about Anchorage. I'm going to be here six months. I'll find out eventually, you know, so you might as well tell me."

"You'll end up dead. Not a lot of cops here to protect you."

"I'm tougher than I look," Phil replied. "Survived a couple of tours down in China. Drug enforcers don't scare me much."

"Yeah, well they scare me. You'll find out anyway, so leave me out of it, will ya?" The kid was panting by now. The hill had taken it out of him.

At least, Phil knew, he'd managed to get a little bit of info on the state of affairs in the city. It was obvious the drug lords did, as speculated, control the lives of at least the lower classes. And in a town one step removed from being a tent city, that meant mostly everyone. His assignment was to expose the dual government in Anchorage, and bring it to the notice of the surviving middle-class in the Midwest, so they could be properly appalled at it.

The upper hill had a few decent-looking restaurants and a couple of nice houses.

"Stop here," Phil said. The view over the city was uninspiring, and the wind was cold, but the Pacific Ocean was magnificent, as always. He turned back to the kid. "What's your name?"

"Reilly."

Sure it is. "Well Reilly, do you think you can take me to one of the farms?"

"Farms?"

"You know the ones I'm talking about. I have satellite photos, so it's not much of a secret."

The kid didn't look happy, but he nodded. "I guess."

"Good. Pick me up at the hotel tomorrow at ten."

Phil paid the kid enough to ensure his appearance the following day. The *Times* would have sprung for a car, but after spending nearly four years in the military destroying fossil-fuel infrastructure to keep the Chinese from spewing more greenhouse emissions into the sky and getting shot at for his trouble, he wasn't much of a car person. Out here, solar power was years from becoming a reality.

‡‡

She didn't fit his image of an opium farmer even remotely. Not too tall, thin, and maybe thirty-five. Dark haired, light skinned and pretty enough without being a classical beauty.

She had opened the door to the farmhouse without asking who was calling, which meant either that she was oblivious of the current social conditions outside her door, or that she had some kind of concealed security system that allowed her to judge the threat posed by visitors. Evidently, she didn't consider a single man and a rickshaw puller to be much of a threat.

Her eyes, however, spoke of a no-nonsense personality and of no time to waste. Although what else she might be doing with her time at this time of year, Phil couldn't imagine.

"Whatever it is," she told him as soon as the door was fully open, "I don't want any." Seeing that he wasn't holding anything that might be considered samples or sales material, she went on, "And I'm a raging atheist without any chance of conversion. My soul was lost years ago, and no matter which religion you represent, no amount of prayer will save me." She moved to close the door.

Phil smiled and held out a hand gently, but placed in such a way that, in order to close the door, she would have to push back his arm. "I'm not a missionary. I'm a reporter."

The relaxed, slightly bored air she'd been affecting vanished. Her eyes immediately locked down and she studied him intently. The first thing she tried was ignorance. "You must have the wrong address. There's nothing about me or my farm that could possibly interest a reporter."

"We both know that isn't true," he replied.

She looked him over again—he could tell that, now that she could see him at close range, she was regretting having opened the door. He was a big guy, and had stayed in shape even after leaving the Marines—and the small scar just beneath his longish brown hair could be seen here. He could never quite decide if it was sinister-looking or not, but hoped it was.

"Where's your camera?"

"What?"

"You say you're a reporter. Where's your camera?"

"At the hotel. I'm not a regular newspaper reporter. I'm doing an article about Anchorage for a special magazine edition of the *Chicago-Detroit Times*. They want to do a full article about the new boomtowns, both in America and in other countries." He shrugged. "I got Anchorage."

"You still haven't told me why you didn't bring a camera." Her arms were still crossed, her expression skeptical, but at least she wasn't trying to close the door.

"Oh, yeah, sorry." Her no-nonsense demeanor had finally gotten to him. "That's because of the way we research these articles. We aim for full cultural immersion. Which means I'm going to be here for the next six months. My method is to get to know the people who are going to be the main characters of my story before writing anything or taking any pictures."

"And you've decided that I'm going to be one of these main characters?"

"Well, no, not yet. I just asked the kid back there to take me to the nearest opium farm, and he brought me here. I would need your okay for that, anyway."

She laughed, short, curt, and to the point. "Yeah, I'd hope so. You can imagine how happy I might be at having you follow me around and take pictures while I cultivate a plant that is illegal except under strict pharmaceutical license everywhere in America. Do you really think I'll let you do something like that? Go away."

"*National Geographic* does it all the time!"

"News for you, man. I'm not a naked little African or South American running around in a desert that wasn't there a few years ago. Or even some Oklahoman in a dust bowl whining about how the government has let half of America dry up. I'm a successful businesswoman. And I don't need you here to ruin it." She gazed at him stonily for a few seconds before proceeding. "And another news flash: you're not the *Geographic*."

She shut the door, pushing him back. He let her.

The next couple of farms were run by people who were cagey at first, but then strangely honored to be included in the article. One of them actually said that he wouldn't mind giving his name and posing for photos. He called his wife and five kids to the sitting room to meet Phil. The girls curtsied cutely and he was offered coffee, lunch and more coffee.

But he left those farms with mixed feelings. Yes, he could write the story as a contrast between the traditional farming values of the old American heartland—these were farming families as Phil had imagined them—and the criminal distribution system they were feeding, and have the article meet all the criteria his editors could want. And he could add a heartwarming, hopeful note about a place where families could still feed children—five of them!—which would truly touch the feelings of people in the lower forty-eight, where professionals could, if careful, raise one child, and the slums were home to starvation and sensationalist rumors of cannibalism.

Or, he could go for the real story. The story of people who'd grown up as something very different. How people who weren't farmers or rugged frontiersmen were getting along, changing the rules, and turning Anchorage into a place that was completely different from the rest of the country. After all, the millions living in the shanties on that hill had arrived in the past five years. And they'd been able to afford the ticket. They probably weren't farmer types. That was the story that would get him the awards.

And he had a feeling that *she* was the key to that particular story.

He spent the next few days attempting to nail down the distribution side of the equation, and quickly discovered some surprising facts. While opium was the biggest game in town, the price and profit margins were nothing like what you got with any natural drug in Chicago. Back in the lower states, the demand to escape from reality was enormous. And the supply of anything—even drugs as obsolete as heroin—was limited, heavily policed. And the synthetic alternatives were a bit like playing Russian Roulette. They were still popular, though.

The whole system was different here: the price of heroin was so low that almost everyone, from rickshaw drivers to executives, could afford their own brand of happiness. Winter, though not as harsh as it once was, was still a serious affair, especially if you lived in a house made of cardboard. Heroin demand went way up in winter. In winter, *everyone* on those streets was in an opiate stupor.

Why did the process work? From what Phil had been able to discern, there was basically one distributor who controlled the drug supply. That, logically, should have meant a high price.

But it didn't. The same heroin made from the same Alaskan opium that was reaching the lower forty-eight with astronomical street values was dirt cheap here in Anchorage. Something simply didn't add up.

Research and bribery had gotten him as far as a mid-level distributor in the supply chain. The guy was an MBA, and his "protection" was essentially an elderly woman at a desk who screened his calls. When Phil, having been unable to get through to him, simply appeared at his office one day, prepared for a showdown with the goons that Reilly was so afraid of, he was met by a smiling red-headed man who'd offered him coffee.

"Where's your muscle?" Phil asked bluntly after exchanging pleasantries.

The guy chuckled softly. "You only need protection when you're running a criminal activity in which large amounts of money are generated. The money from the opium trade in Anchorage, while large, is just enough to cover the expenses of the people working here."

"So why the thugs at street level?" Phil had had run-ins with a couple of them, but nothing too serious.

"They're only there to keep the general population from asking questions. And they're specifically kept from using lethal force. We don't want to start any vendettas—not good business practice."

"So are you going to tell me what's really going on?"

"No. And I'm as far up the chain as you're going to get. So write your story about some other aspect of city life."

He was right. Phil had been effectively stonewalled in every subsequent attempt to go through or around the guy—he wasn't going to get information that way.

He went back to the hotel and sat thinking for a while. He knew that he'd have to find another angle if the story was going to work correctly. He thought he knew what to try tomorrow. And, besides, the girl was pretty.

Same door, but this time it was around seven o'clock, and about a week later. The wind was biting, but he could hardly feel anything other than the unexpected knot in his stomach. He laughed ruefully at himself. *So much for the hardened soldier, the veteran reporter.*

He knocked. And waited. And knocked again.

The door opened a crack. The woman he'd spoken to earlier could be seen in the soft glow coming from inside.

"You again," she said. "What do you want now?"

"Just wanted to see if I could buy you dinner."

"Dinner?"

"Yeah, you know. Like with food and stuff. Maybe candles on the table." Phil had done his research, and knew that she was unmarried and currently unattached, but that her tastes ran towards men. He told the butterflies in his gut that he was only doing this to see what info he could get from her. They didn't believe him.

"I don't think I'm dressed for it," she said, as the door opened. She wasn't—sweat pants and a man's coarse shirt. But then she smiled. "I know you only want information, but nobody in America would ever turn down a free meal, even here in Alaska. Give me five minutes." She turned to go, leaving the door open.

"Aren't you going to tell me your name?"

"You're a reporter, which means professionally nosy. You probably already know my name, my background and the names of my high school sweethearts. I'll go to dinner, but don't bullshit me."

Ouch. She was right. He knew her name and her father's. But that was about it. She'd moved to Alaska six or seven years before, depending on whom one believed, when her father, who'd been there for years, died. Where she'd been before that or what she'd done was anyone's guess.

Fifteen minutes later, she was transformed. Low-riding jeans, a designer t-shirt, hair let down and just the tiniest touch of make-up had Phil reminding himself that, no matter what happened, he couldn't get emotionally involved with an opium farmer who would be central in his article about the pervasive drug culture in Anchorage.

Never fall for the bad guy.

He went all out. Not only had he rented a car—a real petrol-burning, bad for the atmosphere car—but he'd also taken her to the restaurant at the top of the Plaza, one of those slowly rotating jobs that was reputedly the best place in Anchorage. If he'd only wanted to get her to fall for him, he wouldn't have spent the money, but since his ultimate objective was to write the story, and that meant getting the information he needed, it was of the utmost importance to *seem* sincere.

So he asked her about her father.

She smiled. "Everyone thought dad was completely nuts when he bought the farm on the hill. It wasn't a farm back then. Alaska was still too cold to cultivate much of anything. It was just a chunk of rocky ground that spent half the year frozen solid. They basically gave it to him for free."

"When was this?"

"Oh, back before I was born, must have been about twenty-fifty or so. And the land just sat there. Remember, this was when everyone thought that the temperature had gone as high as it would, since we'd gotten the US to cut back greenhouse emissions enough that there was no more growth. The way he used to tell it, my dad was the only one pointing at China. Of course, no one understood atmospheric inertia back then."

Phil nodded. Having gotten her started, he planned to play the "really interested" card for all it was worth. And yet, over the previous hour, he'd discovered a woman of intelligence and spirit notably lacking in the "screw everything—nothing's really worth it" attitude so prevalent down south. He found that he actually cared about her past. Which was something he was going to have to work to avoid.

"So when the drought hit Los Angeles, my parents were on the first plane here. They didn't even bother to sell the house. I still have the deed, although it's worthless now—in the middle of the desert."

"So you were born here."

"Yeah. Back then, you could still drive ten minutes into the countryside and pretend humanity didn't exist. My name, Soledad, means loneliness in Spanish. It was probably a mistake to give me that name." Suddenly, tears welled in her eyes, and the cool competence was replaced by a suddenly vulnerable look.

Phil barely managed to avoid leaning over the table to comfort her. "Why?"

"Mom never got used to the emptiness. She was from LA for Christ's sake! Remember that these people," she gestured at the slowly rotating shanties visible on the hills outside the window, "started arriving in the last ten years. Back when my parents moved here, Anchorage had maybe a quarter million people. And then she got word of the LA riots, and the flooding—she told dad that she wanted to go back, to help her family. Dad refused. Then one day we got word that her parents and her sister had tried to leave the city. Their car was ambushed by water-raiders to the west, and I don't even want to think about what happened, but in the end, all three of them died."

She paused to wipe her eyes. "Why am I even telling you this? You either want to pump me for information or get me into bed and then disappear. Either way, you don't care."

Ouch. A bit too close to home. "That's unfair. I've been listening, haven't I? You're just prejudiced against reporters." He smiled crookedly and this time he did clasp her hand in his.

She shook her head and pulled her hand back. "Mom was distraught. There was nothing we could do to calm her down. Dad thought she just wanted to be alone, so when she said she was going for a walk, he let her."

She took a deep breath. "They found her body washed up on the shore the next day. Coroner said she didn't drown, must have fallen off a cliff. Everyone knew she hadn't fallen, and dad never forgave himself for letting her go. That's when he started drinking." She looked Phil straight in the eye. "I was six years old when this happened, and seventeen when I last saw my father. Went down to Columbia, got a job at an ad agency and worked my way up the ladder. By the time he died I was an account director."

"So what are you doing here?"

"Came to sell the farm, saw the flooded city down there, and realized that dad had been right when he bought this land. And the emptiness, even with five million people, has a call that's in my blood. I never went back to New York."

She looked at him again, as if wondering how much more to tell, and then shrugged. "And besides, I knew that I wouldn't be able to go back and live behind the dykes and in the tunnels again. New York might have managed to hold back the water, but you still get the feeling of living in a cave, with nowhere to go. Here, on the other hand . . ." Her voice trailed off. "Well, it just feels like we're actually building a future."

He took her home in his rented car, and asked her one last question after walking her to the door and telling her how much he'd enjoyed himself. "And the opium? Was your father right about that, too?"

Her laugh was a light, pleasant tinkle. "Of course not." Her eyes twinkled at him. "The opium was my idea. It's been there for about five years. Pleasant dreams," she said as she closed the door behind her.

But it was too late. The hook had been set by her charm, her intelligence and the fact that she was certain that there was a future for America. She was going to be big trouble.

The drive back to his hotel was a somber one.

Five months after their first dinner together, Phil had all the information he needed for the article, and dozens of good photos. He knew the angle he currently had wasn't Pulitzer-worthy, but it would be a competent, interesting article that would be no better or worse than the ones appearing beside it in the issue. How life had changed irrevocably when oceanic expansion caused by increased water temperature, plus melting icecaps, had threatened downtown Anchorage. How the town council had begged the army engineers to place them higher on the priorities list for the dykes, and how they'd been ignored, and could do nothing but watch and grind their teeth as first the big cities like New York and Miami and then cities doomed by the drought in the Southwest were put ahead of them. Nobody had believed the water would run out in San Diego, no matter what the scientists said.

He would tell how they'd had to abandon the city center to the rising ocean. Desolation.

Then hope. The Alaskan Miracle. How, from despondency, hope had arisen when the rising temperatures and changing weather patterns had transformed the cold Alaskan countryside into beautiful, well-watered farmland. How the port city of Anchorage had become, over the course of just a couple of decades, a farming hub where everyone had plenty to eat and lots of water.

He'd wrap it up with a look at what was to come—a mix of hope and trepidation. He would describe Anchorage's future as one of the brightest anywhere in the world, but would temper it with a word of caution regarding the lack of facilities to deal with the exploding population, and the rampant, universal use of drugs derived from the dirt-cheap opium being grown with impunity right here in the countryside surrounding Anchorage.

The whole thing would be illustrated with the life stories of the local protagonists: a farmer, an unemployed addict, a social worker trying to avoid a humanitarian catastrophe. A textbook article.

Bah, he thought. It would be textbook all right, but it wouldn't tell the world what was really happening here. But what was he missing?

The article was ready to write, the notes compiled, and he knew which photos he would recommend to the editor, but he had no intention of leaving just yet.

He lay awake wondering at how completely the last few weeks had changed his life. How the woman beside him had made him view society's morality in a completely new way.

Suddenly, a few lights blinked on the computer screen and a soft alarm chime sounded. Soledad was awake immediately. She jumped out of the bed and began to pull on her jeans.

"What is it?" Phil asked her.

"Perimeter breach in the poppy fields."

Phil knew the ripe poppies could be scored, the lacerations emitting a fluid that, when dried, was the base for heroin. The fluid was always a target for junkies and opportunists.

Soledad typed a couple of commands into the computer, and the screen split into four rectangles, each displaying the feed from a security camera. She quickly took stock of the situation. "Five of them."

"Junkies?" Phil asked.

She looked at him suspiciously, unsure whether he was still trying to get information even now. "Yeah. The dealers would never do this."

"Why not? Sounds like a great way to get free dope."

"We have an agreement," she said, in a voice that meant that further argument would lead to a fight. "These are just some of the people from the shanties trying to get a free fix. One of the few problems with owning the farm nearest the city. We need to stop them before they do something irreversible. The drugs sold down there are very watered down. Now, the essence of the poppy is far from pure, but if they stay long enough . . ."

"Well, I was in the police action in China. I can probably deal with five junkies. Do you think they're armed?"

"Of course not. And don't be silly. You're not going out there. We have ways to deal with this." She picked up the phone and dialed a short number. "Hi, Beth? Soledad here. I have uninvited guests. Five of them. Okay, thanks." She hung up and turned back to Phil. "Now we just sit tight and wait."

"What if they come after the house?"

"It's never happened before, but they'll find the doors are stronger than they look. So are the windows—my dad was a bit paranoid. And there's a shotgun under the bed. So just sit, they'll be here in a few minutes."

"Who will?"

She looked guilty for a second but said nothing.

He just sat, watching the monitor and tensing every time one of the junkies walked toward the house, then relaxing when it turned out to be a false alarm.

Suddenly, the monitors were filled with more people—uniformed people.

"What's going on? Are you being raided by the police?"

Soledad shifted uncomfortably. "Not exactly."

Phil watched the confused milling as the uniformed officers mixed with the junkies in the field. It took a while before he understood the situation. The officers were escorting the junkies off the property. They weren't being too gentle, but they weren't being too rough either. Five minutes later, they were all gone.

Click. The final pieces locked into place, and the potential story went from a competent piece of journalism which would not stand out from its peers to a potential scandal-breaking, Pulitzer-winning bombshell.

"So *that's* why I couldn't get a single lead on the top drug lord in this town. Because the police are in on it too! No wonder they all played dumb no matter how many rounds I bought. And here, I stupidly thought the cops would hate the dealers! So, who is it? The commissioner? One of the captains? Who?"

Soledad looked miserable. She started to speak, then stopped, then started again, but was unable to continue. A single tear rolled down her face. "Look," she said, "it's not any single person. Everyone knows about this."

"And they all turn a blind eye?" Phil's bemusement was beginning to turn into righteous anger. "Everyone in the city's addicted and the whole police force is in on it and nobody does anything?"

"It isn't like that! You're a southerner. You'd never understand."

"Of course not. We try to keep corruption out of public circles down there."

"This isn't corruption! It's for the public good. No one is making any money out of this."

"Sure. I imagine you're giving the heroin away."

She glared at him, hurt. "As a matter of fact, I am, you bastard." Soledad pulled away, refusing to look him in the eyes. "And so is every other poppy farmer around Anchorage."

"Huh? Why?" Phil was confused. He'd just assumed that everyone was making millions off the stuff, just like they had in southeast China when he'd been there. "Hard to believe, when all the farmers live like kings."

She laughed, an ironic bark. "Have you seen the price of *food* these days?" Crying freely now. "Look, when Anchorage began to grow, we began to have a problem with drugs. Real bad stuff, from the labs in Miami. I had just come in from New York, and the mayor had been a friend of my dad's. He came to dinner, and we got to talking about the problem. He explained that drugs cost a fortune, but that the early dark in winter gave a lot of depressed people living on the streets two choices: drugs or suicide. We had the highest per-capita murder rate in the US. And most of it was drug related."

Phil nodded. The same had happened in the southwest when public order had finally become too weak to control the trade coming in from Mexico.

"So I proposed a solution," She concluded. "We would grow our own, fine-tune it to give the user a mild sense of oblivion, enough so that the users would forget their problems, and sell it for peanuts. All we needed was to find the right drug. Eventually, they discovered a genetically modified strain of poppy that could survive the new Alaskan climate from an American company that claimed to only sell it to the pharmaceutical industry. So I became head of Anchorage Pharma, and here we are."

"So you're the drug lord?" Phil couldn't believe it. He'd been with her for months, and had never seen her doing anything not related to work on the farm.

"No. I'm just the name on the papers, because my experience let me pull off the jargon at the meetings. The drug lord, as you call it, would be the mayor."

Phil was stunned beyond words.

She went on. "Look. We've got crime down to negligible levels, no one is starving and the job openings are actually growing at a faster rate than the population for the first time ever. We're in a transition and the drugs are a necessary evil. Even now, we're working on the plan to wean the people off the dope."

"So the ends justify the means, huh?"

Her eyes flashed. "They do when the end is to save lives, yes." The ensuing silence dragged on for minutes. Finally, her red-rimmed eyes looked into his, and she said, "If any of what you said to me over the past few months is true, then you'll never file that story."

He nodded silently. He was a journalist, this could be his biggest ever scoop.

He would have to think about it.

As predicted, he'd been late, but still arrived before Soledad.

A sunset was a sunset, no matter where one was in the world. But something about looking out on the Pacific from an open-faced bar in Anchorage Heights over a late dinner made it special. Poignant, but eerily beautiful.

The office buildings of Old Anchorage jutted out of the water like some cubist version of Venice, the red-tinged water covering streets and most of the lower stories. But these buildings, unlike those in Italy, had not been built to survive in the sea. Especially not in this sea, with its monsoon-driven waves.

And yet, Phil knew, they were inhabited by tens of thousands of migrant workers—people who'd come for the harvest and the planting of winter wheat. Handymen and mechanics had been coming for the past twenty years, but now, with the price of fuel being almost prohibitive, many of the tractors would stay in their sheds—it was cheaper to bring workers in from the south and do everything by hand.

"Phil," Soledad said. "Are you with me?"

"Sorry, just thinking about the people in those buildings."

"What is it with southerners and the shanties? I mean we don't go down south and obsess about your slums, do we?" She smiled to take the sting out of her words, but he knew she meant it. Alaskans were just getting used to the reality of having a city of five million on their coast, and just learning the realities of the migration—they were still sensitive about the poor who lived in those warrens that had once been the old downtown of a much smaller city, and the shantytowns that papered the hills.

Phil smiled back. "I'm from Detroit, you can't really call me a southerner, can you?"

She said nothing, but her eyes twinkled, and he understood that she'd scored on his sensitivities. "Touché," he admitted.

"So, eat your crab. You won't get any better in the lower forty-eight."

"We don't get any at all in the lower forty-eight. The acid's killed them all off."

The bar was just a hole in the wall, peeling yellow paint over plank walls; it looked like something from another century, maybe Key West in the time of Hemingway. But its view of the Pacific from halfway up the hill was simply breathtaking.

"So did you find what you *were* expecting?" Soledad asked him, knowing she was about to lose him once more.

"Quite a bit more, actually," he leered at her. "Amazing hospitality of Alaskan women. Above and beyond the call of duty."

She smiled. "I mean in the city, you pervert."

"Just this," he said, showing her the sheaf of prints and photos in their manila folder.

Her face fell, and the meal was finished in silence, and in both quantity and quality, he had to admit that it was one of the best he'd had in years. And the check came, for both of them, to less than half of what he'd have paid for much poorer fare for one person anywhere in the lower forty-eight.

Finally, she asked him the question that had really been on her mind all through dinner, the one that had burned in the awkward silences, and made their small talk, normally so natural, feel strained.

"So, when are you going to send it in?" she asked, trying to make it sound nonchalant, offhand.

He wasn't fooled. Looking her straight in the eyes, he replied. "The deadline is in a couple of hours. I don't think I'm gonna make it."

She was well aware what that decision meant. What it meant for his career. The sacrifice he was making. "Do you really mean that?"

He nodded. He'd made his choice.

She took him home, tears in her eyes.

Après Moi, le Déluge

by Daniel Stride

THE SUN IS SINKING TOWARDS THE HORIZON AS WE SHUDDER TO A HALT. I check my pocket watch, and nod. Charter steamers from Wilkesland to Rossland are notoriously unreliable, but today we have arrived with time to spare. I scribble a note in my diary; I shall recommend the *D'Urville* to my superiors.

I replace the diary in my breast pocket. "It is a short walk from the port to the château?"

The captain strokes his beard. It dangles thick and black over his chest. "Indeed, Monsieur."

"I have heard of its splendour."

"The Duc's château is a most beautiful building, Monsieur. One of my ancestors worked on its construction."

I collect my briefcase from beneath the seat. "Architect?"

"Labourer, Monsieur."

I hand the man a promissory note, and clamber onto the pier. I do not envy the captain in navigating his exit, not with Rosstown's harbour so packed with traders, steamers, and pleasure craft. The Duc de Rossland's personal barge, the *Venus*, is berthed five hundred metres away. What man paints his vessel pink? Why, the Duc, apparently.

The waterside is a hive of activity this evening. Sweat dripping, muscles straining, the wharf-workers winch Jadeland wool-bales onto the quay. At the other end, arrivals in periwigs cool their buckled heels as they await their luggage.

"Monsieur, may I take your briefcase?"

I flinch. A scrawny fellow stands beside me. Lank blond hair falls across one eye; he scratches a stubbled chin.

I suppress the urge to reach for my pocket pistol. "I shall carry it, thank you."

"You're here for the fête, Monsieur? The fête of farewell?"

He holds out a cloth bag, as if that should mean something.

I frown. "I am."

"I can take you to the château, Monsieur . . ."

"I shall find my own way."

The man pushes back his hair—it needs a good wash. "Monsieur, I appeal to the charity of your purse. I have three children to care for, and the winter night approaches . . ."

"I daresay you should have thought of that *before* you decided to breed. Excuse me."

The cobblestone road forks sharply. To the left lies Rosstown proper, with its mills, dens, and boarding houses, a place choked with soot and teeming with hungry mouths. To the right, through a thicket of beech, the way winds gently up a hill. Right it is. I follow a line of periwigged noblemen and their servants. Shoving a fern frond from my path, I catch sight of the magnificent snow-capped peak of Mont Erebus, its slopes tinted blood-red by the setting sun.

One cannot easily forget the château of the Duc de Rossland. Fashioned from local limestone two centuries ago, its south wing alone dwarfs any other building on the island. One hundred windows, each glazed eight times over, glare out towards the Ross Sea. No mystery that folk flock from across the Antarctic Isles to see this last wonder of the world.

Outside the gates, the Duc has set up a blue-and-gold marquee. All manner of people and paupers swarm about, many clasping bags like the beggar's.

"Food, Monsieur?"

I am addressed by a stout and ruddy woman of late-middle years. Clad in a white woollen apron, she shoves loaves and jars into bags.

I frown. "What is this?"

The woman's smile reveals two missing front teeth. "Tradition, Monsieur. Are you a visitor to Rossland?"

"I am. And I am disappointed to see such wastage. Why are these items not in the Duc's winter cellar?"

The smile vanishes. "Monsieur, every year at the fête of farewell, the Duc gives away food to the masses. Six months of night take their toll."

"They should be *allowed* to take their toll."

"Not if His Grace can help it. When the night is darkest, he slips on his fur coat, and ventures forth to Rosstown's hovels, delivering parcels in person. Now, Monsieur, here's a bag for you. Two rye loaves, a rind of Ross Cheese, and a jar each of pickled herring and cabbage. Compliments from Rossland."

My mouth twists. I turn away.

‡‡

I follow a red-brick path to the main doors, past the Duc's topiary penguins. Inside the entrance hall, I shrug off my travelling overcoat—necessary at this time of year—and pass it to a footman. This one wears a crimson sash over a jacket of verdant green; the face beneath the periwig is young and bright-eyed.

"Your invitation, Monsieur?"

He inspects the card. My name is inscribed in silver ink.

"There are buffet tables in the banquet hall, Monsieur." He gestures towards a flight of stairs. "Whatever is in the briefcase?"

I smile. "You will find out soon enough."

I slip the invitation back into my breast pocket, and follow the sound of the cellos.

The envy of West Antarctica, watercolours and oils line the panelled walls, each depicting the last stands of battles long ago. Obsidian and marble statues of the Duc's ancestors peer out from alcoves, haughty in stone as in life. I pay them only brief glances. I am a coal merchant, from a long line of coal merchants. I can never aspire to the ranks of those whose forebears cut across these Isles with iron and blood, at the dawn of Antarctica's Green Age. But neither am I courtier or peasant. My way is the future.

The banquet hall's doors have been thrown open. I blink; from chequerboard floor to vaulted ceiling, the room is bright as the midsummer sun. In one corner, velvet-clad musicians play a fearsome tune, the cellists hounding their strings until the rosin flies. Beneath the crystal chandelier and its dozens of brilliant candles, a score of mad dancers essay to keep up. Then, without warning, the music stops. Some dancers cannot stop in time, and are clapped off the floor. The tune resumes, with those who remain.

At the far end, His Grace has erected tables laden with pheasant, venison, fish, and lamb—each dish smothered with thick sauces. There are bowls filled with all manner of fruits, from the furry monstrosities of Jadeland to offerings from the northern borders of Hornland. There are rich red wines from the Great Peninsula, salads drenched in vinaigrette dressing, and strong malodorous cheeses. As I abstain from meat, I migrate to the salad table, keeping an eye out for my promised contact. Alas, I see only the periwigs of the great and the good, the nobility of the Antarctic Isles chirping like grasshoppers as the six month night closes in.

The dressing is over-sweet, but the lettuce is crisp and cold as one could hope for. Not three metres away, a man in an ill-fitting waistcoat recites doggerel to a trio of full-bosomed ladies. The fellow is some fifty years; with his double chin and red nose, he is a fountain of low and boisterous humour. With any luck, the Duc will throw him out before he causes mischief.

I finish the salad, and inspect my pocket watch. I groan. My contact should have met me ten minutes ago, at the agreed upon location. I have travelled far on important business. Nay, critical business; the future of the Isles rests in my brain and my briefcase. And dare I say it, punctuality matters. I note in my diary to lodge a complaint.

"Monsieur?"

A footman rushes through the throng towards me, a gloved hand holding aloft a silver tray. He kneels. "For you, Monsieur."

I frown, and lift a letter from the tray. "What is this?"

"It was left for you, Monsieur. A messenger arrived not fifteen minutes ago."

I break the seal, and read. I recognise my contact's spidery hand.

Cannot make it tonight. Have an infernal fever. - D

I tear the letter in twain.

The footman blinks. "Monsieur?"

I drop the pieces onto the tray. "Go."

Three smiling periwigs eye me over their wine glasses. I grit my teeth, and turn back to the table. Let them titter. They do not know it, but I, a lowly merchant, hold their lives in my hand.

I resist the urge to storm out the fête, out into the twilight gloom. No, that would be unseemly. I must present a positive image for the company. I fetch a lemon cordial. Its cool, tart bite refreshes me and clears my head.

"We'll drink up all day and lech up all night, so let's all give thanks for the life-giving light!"

The doggerel ends amid applause. I sip my drink, reflecting that neither money nor breeding can buy taste. The fat poet belches, to much laughter.

"Now, ladies," he says, "if you don't mind, I must sample some cordial. I can't just drink wine, you know, else I shall fall asleep before the big moment. My father did that one year, and look what happened to him!"

He slaps his belly, and waddles over to the drinks table. He is reaching for the silver pitcher when our eyes meet.

"My goodness, Monsieur! With a face like that, you'd think this winter was never-ending! Tell me, what's the matter?"

"I *was* to meet a Rossland contact tonight to discuss important business matters before broaching them with the Duc. . . . It is a most sensitive point."

The man's chins wobble. "Your contact couldn't make it?"

"Correct, Monsieur. Rendering my evening wasted."

The wastrel laughs. A deep belly laugh.

"Begging your pardon, Monsieur." I fight the urge to snap. "What is so funny?"

"You have had a most successful evening."

I slam my half-finished cordial onto the table. "How . . ."

"You have cut the middle man from your plans. I *am* the Duc."

My eyes widen. *This* was the most powerful lord in the Isles? But of course: he paints his pleasure barge pink. Silently cursing my idiocy, I drop to my knees.

"My apologies, Your Grace. I failed to recognise you."

"Not to worry, Monsieur, not to worry. Come, let us go to my private balcony. There you may tell me of this sensitive issue."

I rise to my feet, and collect my briefcase. "As you wish, Your Grace."

The Duc leads me from the banquet hall. He turns to shoo back the trailing line of periwigs and servants.

"Sincere apologies, good folk, but I need to discuss business. I am just going outside, and may be some time."

There is a collective groan from the hordes.

"But we need you to perform the farewell ceremony!"

"And finish your ever-so-saucy verses!"

The Duc smiles. "I shall return in time to both perform the ceremony and finish *several* poems."

The populace cheers.

"Now enjoy yourselves. There's plenty of food left, and I'd hate to have to eat it all myself. Go!"

He winks at me.

The Duc moves swiftly for a big man; I keep a brisk pace in his wake. He leads me up stairs lined with green carpet. A succession of oil portraits grace the walls.

"See that one?"

He points at the last portrait on the right. It depicts a pudgy blond-haired boy, no more than six, leading a tame emperor penguin chick with a ribbon.

"My youngest son. He'll be learning to ride a horse next year!"

I frown. "But Your Grace is a bachelor, famously so."

"I am indeed."

"But . . . oh."

The Duc chuckles. "No fear. Are you married? Never seen the point myself."

My mouth twists. "Yes, Your Grace. I have been married these ten years."

"Children?"

"None, Your Grace."

He stops, and looks at me. His face sags. "I am so sorry, Monsieur. Too much wine—I should not have asked . . ."

"It is by choice, Your Grace."

He makes no reply.

The next set of doors lead through to a sunroom. Thick woollen curtains embroidered with heraldic golden penguins hang from every wall and window: put away during the six month day, my contact tells me they are revived ahead of the six month night. One such curtain hides the door to the Duc's private balcony.

It is smaller and more austere than I expected. Fashioned from the same grey limestone as the rest of the château, there is only a low seating bench. Looking out from the railing, one sees a rugged stretch of land, infested with ferns and sloping sharply towards the coast. Beyond that lie the dark and melancholy waters of the Ross Sea. I estimate there is still half an hour before the sun disappears.

The Duc sits. He is breathing heavily. "So what is it, Monsieur? Hmmm?"

"Your Grace, I represent the Amundsen Mining Company."

He grins, and slaps his thigh. "My seneschal shall approve your licence next week, Monsieur. Worry not."

I shake my head. "No, Your Grace. Our survey team has returned an updated estimate of Rossland's remaining coal reserves."

"And?"

I lean against the railing. It is cold beneath my fingers. "Your Grace, previous estimates are wrong. Catastrophically so."

"How catastrophic?"

"Less than thirty years of reserves remain, at current consumption. Of course, your population continues to increase, so that is an optimistic estimate."

"I see. I am no businessman—never had a head for numbers—but you are a coal merchant. Wouldn't a shortage mean higher coal prices, and thus more gold for you? If so, why are you complaining to me?"

"Your Grace is correct. In the short term, Amundsen Mining would benefit greatly. Unfortunately, your way of life also depends on coal—it is your shield against the six month night—and a prolonged shortage would destroy you."

"Hornland, Jadeland, and Wilkesland manage well enough."

"Hornland, Jadeland, and Wilkesland have forests, Your Grace. Since the dawn of the Green Age, my people have burnt wood, supplemented these past centuries by the far more efficient Rossland coal. You are on an island—a *small* island, Your Grace—and even were every millimetre of your realm covered in trees, you would still lack fuel for your present population."

"Can we not import your wood, like you import our coal?"

"Paid for by what, Your Grace? You sell the Isles coal and finished goods made with coal. Without it, you have nothing. Besides, even if the other duchies were minded to gift you wood, they cannot ship the needed load over treacherous winter seas."

The Duc thins his lips. "A pickle."

"As for me, if you fall, you take the coal merchants with you. Survival trumps profit, Your Grace."

"A flea needs a host."

I grimace. "One way of putting it, Your Grace. I have the reports in my briefcase if you wish to see them—they explain the situation better than I."

The Duc flicks his hand. "Don't. No head for numbers, remember? Show these to my seneschal and my brother Francis—the next in line, if you care about such things. He's the accountant in the family. So what do you want me to do?"

"I have three proposals, Your Grace. The details of two of them accompany the reports, while the third is based on recent observation . . ."

"Damn it, Monsieur. Tell me plainly what I must do, else I'll throw you off this balcony and let my dogs devour your carcass."

I sigh. I am no Rosslander; my contact knows this man better than I. Still, I pride myself on facing hard facts.

"Your Grace, you must cease exporting coal. Stockpile it beneath your château, under lock and key. Arm your guards."

The Duc frowns. "That would antagonise the other duchies."

"They have forests, Your Grace. They shall survive."

"Then what about paying for imports? We are a net importer of food. That, I do remember."

"You must make do, Your Grace."

"Indeed. I suppose existing greenhouses can be co-opted and expanded. I'll talk with Francis about it. What is the second proposal?"

"You must strictly regulate coal usage within Rossland. No one may use more than the decreed limit, on pain of the gallows."

"A most unusual suggestion, Monsieur. It would mean death for many of the poorer Rosstown folk during late winter."

"A price you must pay, Your Grace."

The Duc twitches. "I suppose I could house them here. The château gets cold, of course, very cold, and it'll be insanely cramped, but . . ."

I shake my head. "I do not recommend it, Your Grace. My third proposal—one you may find distasteful, but which I assure you is absolutely necessary—is that you stop gifting winter food to your subjects."

The Duc's eyes widen. "I do not believe my ears! You wish a famine upon my people?"

"A famine will reduce Rossland's overpopulation to more sustainable levels, Your Grace. It will allow your precious coal reserves to last longer."

"A pox upon the reserves!"

"There will be short-term pain, but in the future, once things have stabilised . . ."

Beneath the full-length wig, his face flushes beetroot. "Curse your future! I'll throw you from this balcony right now!"

The Duc steps towards me. I stand my ground.

"Your Grace, there is no alternative."

"There's always an alternative."

"Like what, Your Grace?"

"Like . . ." The Duc suddenly laughs. "I have it—we could limit the number of children per family. Yes, that's it! We're saved!"

"Your Grace, this is too little too late. You must reduce your population immediately. Your choice is either starvation now, or the end of Rossland thirty years hence."

He stares blankly out to sea. I follow his gaze. The sun continues to sink below the horizon.

"We've been here before, I think."

"Your Grace?"

"Many years ago, when I was a boy, I liked to spend winter in the library. I could not go outside, obviously, and Francis made a dull companion even then. Among those big beautiful books, I imagined myself an adventurer, or a pirate, or a coal smuggler." He grins mischievously. "One day, I ran across some ancient texts. Historical records laid down by an ancestor of mine. Do you know how the Green Age came to be?"

I shake my head. "History is not my area, nor my concern, Your Grace. We must always and only think of the future. Perhaps if I spoke to your brother . . ."

"The text mentioned a time of calamity, when all that was precious ran short. A decline: long, slow, and painful, punctuated by crises and doom. But even as one door shut, another opened. The ice melted from the Antarctic Isles, birthing the Green Age—and here we are today. What shall be shall be."

"What shall be is the end of you."

"Perhaps." He smiles. "Perhaps we face catastrophe. Yet, maybe in time East Antarctica shall also be free of ice, revealing its mysteries. Then men like us shall stand ten thousand years hence, having this conversation again."

"Your Grace, there shall be no men in ten thousand years. We may delay the day of doom, yet there will come a time when the last of our race closes his eyes, and our rule on Earth is ended."

"The Earth shall not miss us, I should think. You wish to prolong the human race, Monsieur? Just as you would prolong Rossland?"

"Beyond all else, Your Grace."

"I would not purchase such survival with misery and suffering. If I must go into the dark, I will go with a wine in my hand and a song in my heart. I am not a clever man, Monsieur, but I know life is meant to be enjoyed and not merely lived.

A life lived for life's sake strikes me as a weak and miserable thing. And now the sun sets. I must return to perform the ceremonies. Good night, Monsieur."

I have no choice. He will not listen to reason, nor follow the path required to save Rossland. His brother will, but by the time he inherits it will be too late. I must do it. I must. For the future of the world.

As the Duc turns to go back through the door, I pull the pistol from my pocket, and shoot him. Once, twice, thrice, in his broad back. And once in the head, to be sure.

The deed done, I sit on the balcony bench. The Duc's blood pools around his corpse, soaking into the curtain. A breeze, light and chill, passes over; my eyes turn towards the horizon.

By the time they find us, the sun has set.

THE CUPERTINIANS

BY DAMIAN MACRAE

As Gibbon walked along the narrow, forest trail, he reflected on the day. The deal had gone well and his coin pouch now had a reassuring heft. However, considering the questionable quality of the goods, Gibbon thought it prudent to move on. A few nights sleeping rough on the trail from Zehun to Port Hemskirk was preferable to uncomfortable questions from the Burley boys. Ships of all shapes and sizes left daily from the busy port and it would be an easy matter to arrange transport to New Hobart with its fine food, luxury hotels, electric conveniences. Within a week, he could be sitting by a warm fire sipping the finest Flinders wine. The unpleasantness of the past few months would become but a distant memory.

The trail rose steeply towards a small summit. Trees which had hugged so closely all afternoon, now opened up to reveal a stunning vista of hundreds of small rugged islands scattered across the sea. Above him and to the left rose towering, cloud capped mountains while in the far distance Gibbon could just make out the smoky haze above Port Hemskirk. Satisfied with today's progress, Gibbon thought this grassy clearing and its expansive views would make an excellent location for camp. He began to wander the clearing (making sure to avoid several obnoxious scat piles), collecting wood.

Twilight falling, Gibbon sat down and prepared to light his fire. The heat would be a welcome balm to his tired muscles. Glancing back towards Zehun, he observed with some alarm a small fire flickering into life on the far side of the valley. This was unusual as most travellers chose to wait for the weekly ferry. Could the Burley boys have tested a sample already? Gibbon frowned. In all likelihood, a vindictive purpose was guiding this stranger. He took solace in the fact that at least they were not mounted, else they would have effortlessly overtaken him hours ago.

Deciding to forego the fire lest he risk discovery, Gibbon considered his new circumstances. Could he make it to Port Hemskirk before capture? Surely if an enthusiastic pace was maintained he would stay ahead, constantly out of reach? This idea was appealing in many respects, not the least of which was a general similarity to his previous plan. Yes, thought Gibbon, a good night's rest and an early start will see me to a deserved conclusion.

Synchronous with the rising moon, the rowdy night life of a dense temperate forest awoke. Gibbon's clearing was assaulted on all sides by constant noise and commotion. Animals of unknown character thumped, crunched and screeched their way through the dense undergrowth surrounding his small camp. Sleep, elusive at first, came slow and fitfully.

In the deep of the night a loud and particularly malevolent screech jarred Gibbon awake. He sat up, rubbing his sore back and looked across the moonlit clearing. An owl sitting on a high branch watched with a bemused expression and large unblinking eyes. Gibbon glared as it gave a satisfied hoot and flapped noiselessly away. He lay back down to begin the slow descent into sleep.

Later, he was awoken again by the sounds of intense mastication. The forest now quiet, he sleepily watched an enormous four legged creature amble peacefully across the moonlit clearing. Taller than a horse, with a stocky and powerful body, it stopped every few steps to eat the choicest grass fronds. At the edge of the clearing it pushed on into the undergrowth, oblivious to the cracking branches as it disappeared deep into the forest.

The first rays of dawn saw a bleary-eyed Gibbon striding purposefully towards Port Hemskirk. The Western Isles was the most remote and least populated province of Tasmania. It consisted of a narrow strip of land, hemmed in by mountains to the east and ocean to the west. Dense forests, clear cold water and abandoned mines provided timber, fish and shiny metals. Hundreds of scattered islands, deep fjords and small coves provided havens for pirates and smugglers. They were constantly finding new and resourceful ways to get these valuable goods past the Tasmanian Navy and their tariffs. With no roads across the mountains, all passengers and goods went via Port Hemskirk. Gibbon was contemplating if he wanted to pay extra for a private cabin and premium victuals when he noticed a stationary cart at the looming fork in the road.

As Gibbon approached he observed a rotund fellow with a circular face and obnoxiously happy demeanour swinging his legs from the back of the cart like a fool. The small cart had several hessian bags piled around some wooden crates. One bag was open and overflowing with apples. An empty harness swung despondently from the cart. Of the pony, mule or other beast of burden, there was no sign.

The rotund fool spoke first. "Good morning, stranger."

"Hello, good sir. My name is Gibbon, and it is certainly a fine day to meet another traveller!"

The man glanced at the sky, thinking for a moment before nodding in agreement and replying, "Well hello, Gibbon." He jumped down from the cart and walked up to him, shaking his hand. "My name is Fox. I don't often meet anyone on this trail. Most choose to forsake the wonders of our glorious forests and opt instead for the ferry."

"I couldn't agree more. Just last night I was amazed by the intense variety of noises made by animals at night." He paused. "Yet, perhaps there is something to be said for a smooth sail down the coast, even if it does weigh heavy on the purse. Some have even suggested this trail is frequented by bandits and other unsavoury types."

Fox stared briefly towards to coast. "There is a risk on the road, I won't deny it. Though the real dangers are above us in the mountains. Also don't forget those same unsavoury types can torment the ferry. In addition to the storms, sharks, water spouts, cantankerous whales and the other uncountable dangers of the blue void. No, taking the good and bad I would prefer a land journey every time!"

"No doubt you speak from experience."

Both men gazed down at the ocean in silence. On the horizon Gibbon saw a white smudge. It soon resolved into a ship, flying downwind towards Port Hemskirk. Fox saw it as well and pointed. "Speaking of the ferry, there it is now. I wonder what foul customer or circumstance drove Jones to leave a day early?"

Gibbon's face betrayed nothing, but inside his heart sank. He had a pretty good idea why Jones was "convinced" to leave early and it did not bode well for his private cabin on a Harvest Moon clipper. Quickly composing himself he replied, "Some trifling non-issue I am sure. Are you heading to Port Hemskirk? I can't help notice you have no horse or pony."

A smile quickly passed over Fox's face as he replied, "Fate has not been kind to me. This morning I awoke to find my loyal beast had fled in the night. I know not the reason why, I always treated him kindly." Fox turned to look along the fork in the trail to the mountains beyond. "My destination is a compound sitting beyond that mountain peak and I now wonder how it shall be managed."

The locals in Zehun had talked to Gibbon in tedious detail about the mountains. No one went up there. Nothing but certain injury or death for the traveller foolish enough to consider it, they said. It was full of unmarked mine shafts and dangerous wildlife. If you managed to avoid or sneak past those dangers, ancient clockwork traps called Guardians would surely get you. Left behind from long forgotten conflicts, Guardians were scattered across the mountain passes and had claimed many an intrepid explorer in the early days of settlement.

Gibbon looked along the path which quickly disappeared between tall trees and ferns. Above, the mountain pass was lost in dense fog.

"Do you travel regularly to this compound? I have heard disturbing stories about these mountains."

"Those stories are for the most part true," Fox replied. "But my . . . family . . . has been making deliveries in these parts for generations. I know the way and possess the necessary talismans and passwords to bypass the Guardians."

Gibbon turned back to the ocean, a sour expression sitting on his face as he watched the ship raise even more sail. Forcing himself to smile and turning towards Fox he said, "Perhaps your misfortune could serve us both. I have long heard of the majestic mountains which tower over the Western Isles. It was only warnings of certain and painful death which turned me away. Would you accept a guest on your delivery? In exchange I could share the burden of the cart."

"You are too generous, I could never impose such a request on my closest friends, let alone a new acquaintance such as yourself. Besides, I have no spare coin to pay you."

Gibbon coughed before beaming back at Fox. "Nonsense, I would not expect a large payment. Good food and perhaps a small trinket is ample."

Fox considered for a few seconds. "Well, you seem a generous fellow and I am sure we can work something out." He then strapped into the cart's harness and slowly began to pull it up the path. "I will take the first shift. Now, let us make haste before any more of this day is wasted."

Gibbon did not like the vague terms he was agreeing to, but at any moment his pursuer may come round the bend. He turned with a resigned sigh and followed Fox up the trail, disappearing past ferns bigger than houses.

It was cool under the dense forest canopy and the path was easy and well worn. They crossed several small creeks and Gibbon would watch large trout dart into the depths as the cart noisily splashed through their home. At one point he even saw some sort of otter, but with a duck's bill where the mouth should be. It was gone before he could point it out to Fox. By midday, the trail steepened and they began to climb the mountain proper. Fox declared this was an opportune time to take a break. He handed Gibbon an apple and some cheese. They ate their lunch looking down over the glittering fjords, bays and inlets of the Western Isles. Of the mysterious pursuer, there was no sign.

After lunch, Fox announced it was time to swap cart duties. Gibbon looked suspiciously at the now very steep trail ahead, and the smooth gently undulating section they had just covered.

"I notice the hard work now begins. No doubt we will be swapping regularly to avoid exhaustion?" Gibbon enquired.

"Of course good friend, in fact I expect we will reach the first camp site soon," Fox assured.

Mollified, Gibbon stepped into the harness and waited as Fox fussed over the various belts, straps and linkages. After a moment he stepped back and announced, "Perfect, it fits like it was made for you!"

"Are you sure, it feels quite tight and my arms are tangled," Gibbon replied.

"Don't worry yourself, your body will quickly adjust. Now let us be away, respite and a warm fire await."

Gibbon reluctantly followed, harness jingling as the cart dragged behind him.

It was late afternoon as Gibbon and Fox pulled up at the remains of an ancient wall. Only a small section was still standing, the rest a line of rubble extending off into the undergrowth. Strangely, no vegetation grew on any of it. Ancient grooves hinted there was once a gate. With no obvious impediment Gibbon started to move forward, giving Fox a sharp look to convey his view on the cart sharing situation.

Fox leaped in front of him. "Stop my friend, you cannot pass the threshold without a valid talisman."

"The gate is long since gone, surely we can pass unmolested?"

"Many foolhardy souls have made that mistake, look beyond and you will see why."

Still strapped into the cart, Gibbon carefully shuffled forward. Past the wall, standing amongst the trees on either side of the path were two imposing stone pillars. Each was taller than a man and capped by a glassy, black sphere. From within the left hand sphere, a small red light flashed every few moments. Gibbon could sense a dispassionate malice emanating from within. The right-hand pillar flashed no light and he knew it was dead inside.

"Are those Guardians?"

"Yes," Fox replied. "They enthusiastically deny entry to any transgressor." Fox picked up a small rock and tossed it up the trail. The sphere on the left hand Guardian spun and swivelled to track the rock as it sailed through the air. A red beam shot out and the rock promptly exploded in a cloud of dust. The dome spun and snapped back into position with a desultory click. Gibbon had seen devious traps and automatic turrets in his travels. They tended to be cantankerous and non-discriminatory, often claiming the owner as victim.

"I have never seen a clockwork turret work so quickly before, or strike out with light itself."

"They are not clockwork," Fox said. "My grandfather once told me they possessed 'logic engines' which could think like a man. I don't know if it's true, only that they attack any without a talisman." Fox gazed at the Guardians with a small smile, almost proud of the pillars of death up ahead.

"They must be ancient, how can they still be working?"

"I don't know. Many have gone cold over the centuries. Perhaps in the future, as old stories become superstitions the lure of salvage and riches will send some brave or foolhardy souls up here to test them." Fox paused for a moment, presumably upset at the eventual prospect of open access to his mountain. "Anyhow, we must push on in order to reach the first camp site before dark. I must admit your pace with the cart is a little lacking, no doubt you will redouble your efforts." Before Gibbon could formulate a suitable rejoinder Fox continued, "Don't be so glum, in time you will improve! Now stay still while I put this on, you don't want to be mistaken for a miscreant by the Guardian." Fox pulled two necklaces from his jacket and placed one over Gibbon's head. They were identical with a delicate, circular silver pendant hanging from a crude chain. It almost looked like an apple with a small bite taken from it. Fox strode confidently forward, signalling to follow. Gibbon waited until it was clear that Fox had passed unmolested before moving forward. The smooth blank sphere rotated and tracked him for a few seconds. After a few brief flashes of red it clicked back to resume its timeless vigil.

They reached the campsite just before sunset. It was beneath another gate similar to the one they had just left. Well-used campfire remains suggested Fox must come this way regularly. As before, two Guardians stood vigil just beyond the threshold. Gibbon noted with some trepidation that both had a red light steadily flashing.

"What a day," Gibbon announced. "I'm exhausted and it's clear you played a little joke on me but I am not one to hold a grudge. If you could be so kind as to untangle me from this wretched harness, I shall take a short nap while you light the fire and prepare dinner. I couldn't help but notice some choice items in the cart. That red wine would go well with the Shepherd's pie. And for dessert it would be amiss not to try the apple and cinnamon tart."

Chuckling to himself, Fox began to unstrap Gibbon from his harness. "I must apologise, I promise we will share the burdens of this journey more equally tomorrow. As for the food, you misunderstand. Those supplies are part of the consignment and must remain unmolested." Fox unclipped the last buckle, releasing him from the cart. "Still, I promised good food and no one can say Fox is not a man of his word. If you can delay your deserved rest and start a fire I shall prepare our meal."

Gibbon thought to protest but lacked the enthusiasm so began sulkily walking around the surrounding trees. Any sticks not dry enough for a fire, he tossed towards the Guardians and watched with satisfaction as they competed to destroy it first. After the third stick, they began tracking him, red lights flashing in time with his heartbeat. Gibbon fumbled for the pendant, holding it high above his head as he quickly retreated back to camp.

The roaring campfire was making satisfied pops and crackles as Gibbon sat down with an exhausted sigh. Fox wandered back from the cart with a plate of old bread and some slightly suspicious looking cheese. Gibbon glanced at Fox's plate which contained a generous serving of pie, fresh bread and pickled vegetables. Fox noticed his evident disappointment, explaining, "Sorry my friend, but there is only enough for one. Furthermore, I have been looking forward to this meal all day. Up until now, you had no knowledge of its existence and thus your dissatisfaction will necessarily be limited."

"Perhaps we could share the meal and both take comfort in its provisions," Gibbon suggested.

"That would be a superficial solution only leading to disappointment for both of us." Fox tasted the pie before continuing, "I suggest taking solace and gratitude for what you have received rather than what you have not."

Gibbon could only silently rage as he chewed on the tough bread.

Fox took another bite of pie. "Perhaps as compensation I might volunteer a new arrangement?"

Gibbon silently nodded assent to continue.

"If you agree to continue pulling the cart I will share half my payment with you. The rate is generous and the journey nearly complete."

Gibbon remained silent for a minute, considering his options before replying. "Of course. You have been more than generous and I accept your offer whole-heartedly. Now let us finish eating so I can get a good night's rest."

Fox gave one of his knowing smiles and nodded in agreement. After dinner, there was idle conversation one would expect around a fire in the wilderness. How far away the stars were, what nature of beast made that noise, and so forth. Eventually, Fox removed blankets from the cart and they both retired for the night.

Fox was woken at dawn by the creaking cart as Gibbon pulled it past his head and through the gate. "Don't stir, my good friend," Gibbon breezily announced. "Your kind offer last night has induced me to make an early start. Why don't you sleep in and catch up in your own time?"

Fox lay back down with a groggy smile before snapping back awake as if from a nightmare. He frantically checked pockets and pack for the pendant, but it was gone. Realisation slowly dawning, he looked up to see Gibbon smiling from the far side of the Guardians holding two pendants from his hand. Fox began cursing but Gibbon had already turned, pulling the cart up the mountain.

Eventually, Fox's loud exclamations diminished and fell silent.

"Perhaps that villain will think twice in the future before taking advantage of an innocent traveller," Gibbon said to himself. The day wore on with him pulling the cart at a comfortable, sedate pace. The trail began a series of switchbacks as it climbed towards the mountain pass. The trees became stunted and soon the only vegetation of note was small, mossy plants growing in and around a rocky scree. Gibbon reached the pass at lunchtime. Deciding he had achieved enough for the day, he set up camp among a scattering of large boulders. Beyond the pass, thick fog and cloud blocked his view. Westward, he could still see all the way down the trail. Islands dotted the calm, blue ocean. Large ships were small dark specks with flashes of white canvas. Gibbon helped himself to the cart's generous provisions, made a small fire and settled in to enjoy a lazy afternoon.

The next few days passed in much the same manner. Gibbon started late and finished early. At no point did he needlessly exert himself to a faster pace. The only task he set to with enthusiasm was meal preparation. These were many, varied and sumptuous, and he quickly dismissed thoughts of any potential consequences from these actions. The mountain plateau was constantly blanketed in thick fog. Sometimes, Gibbon would catch glimpses of grassy tussocks and scattered shallow lakes before the cloud and fog rolled back. Occasionally he would pass a lifeless Guardian, some even missing their glassy spheres.

On the fourth day, just as Gibbon began to think that Fox had played yet another prank, the fog lifted and a large structure came into view. It was made of imposing smooth stone walls large enough to enclose a town. There were no battlements or features of any kind except for a steel gate, standing slightly ajar. It was clearly ancient, rusty and haphazardly patched with steel pieces of differing ages and colours. Slightly back from the gate a small, wooden hut stood alone. Gibbon could see or hear no signs of life from within the compound. In the far distance a small herd of goats wandered, bells tinkling as they grazed.

Gibbon approached cautiously, making sure his pendant was clearly visible. At the wooden hut he stopped and unhitched from the cart. Inside was a scattering of empty crates and sacks, no doubt where Fox made his deliveries. Sitting on a table was a small coin pouch and handwritten note. The wavering scrawl was barely legible, although the symbols for "tardiness" and "reduced payment" had been carefully drawn. Gibbon emptied the coin pouch, adding the contents to his own. The compound still remained silent. He walked closer to the gate, loudly announcing, "I graciously accept the deposit for this delivery. I am of course obliged to wait for full payment. Perhaps you have lodging and a warm meal for a weary traveller?" There was no response. In the distance, Gibbon noticed the goats had stopped grazing and were all staring at him. Feeling stupid, he returned to the hut.

Morning passed into a sunny afternoon with no sign of life from the compound. Building up courage, Gibbon set himself to walking around the compound at a respectable and safe distance. It was square, one hundred paces to a side and made from a smooth, highly polished stone. He noticed the occasional crack that had not being repaired. There were no windows or any other gates. On each corner, Gibbon found a small circular stone base big enough to support a Guardian. Of the Guardians themselves there was no sign. Back at the hut, Gibbon set about making a small fire and a modest meal. There were no objections or acknowledgment from the compound, even when he opened a bottle of the vintage red.

The following morning, Gibbon groggily awoke to the sound of tiny bells. Sitting up, he frightened and scattered the herd of goats. Several of the smarter ones made sure to drag a bag of food with them as they retreated from the gesticulating human. Gibbon looked with dismay at the mess. Most of the supplies were gone. Worse, they had favoured the choicest items. He tidied and repacked as best he could, constantly looking back to the compound for signs of disapproval, or worse, demands for a refund. Except for the quiet rustle of a breeze flowing through the ajar gate, it remained silent.

Stepping onto the path facing the compound, Gibbon loudly announced his honourable intentions. He reminded them that delivery was made in full yesterday and there could be no discount for the goat incident. Furthermore, he now intended to enter the compound and claim full payment. Taking the silent reply as assent, Gibbon boldly stepped through the gate.

Inside were rows of unkempt garden beds clogged with weeds. Two large, glass greenhouses flanked a small, squat stone building with a single iron door. No threats or admonitions were issued. No Guardians rose up from the ground. The place looked abandoned, but someone had left that coin pouch and letter. Gibbon moved into the first greenhouse. He slowly opened the door to be assaulted by a wave of humid air and a cloud of insects. Inside was overflowing with different plants, flowers and ferns all fighting with each other to dominate the enclosed space. When it was clear no one was inside, Gibbon moved onto the second greenhouse.

By contrast, its gardens were well kept and under control. They were also completely ornamental with no edible fruits or vegetables. He wandered through in awe. Ferns, flowers, water features, rock structures and orchids. It was beautiful, and yet wholly impractical. In the centre was a garden bed containing a small headstone and overflowing with tiny blue flowers. Facing the garden bed was a man slumped in a chair. Gibbon made several discrete coughs. After no response he stepped forward. The man had taut, papery skin and a shaved head. Congealed blood and mucus dribbled from his nose, his eyes rolled back showing only white. The man was dead, no more than two or three days gone. Not one for deep self-reflection and contemplation, Gibbon was perturbed only briefly. A simple funeral service could be arranged. With no one left alive, he could decide on suitable compensation for his efforts. Natural justice demanded it!

Several hours later Gibbon stood beside two graves. Unfortunately most of the blue flowers were now trampled, but he was sure they would grow back. The old headstone was engraved in a strange unintelligible script and a number which made no sense (3023?). For the old man, Gibbon built a small rock cairn. "I never knew your name let alone your deeds. But I will ensure your memory is not tarnished by rumours of late and vacillating payments. Your reputation is safe with me!"

Funeral services discharged, Gibbon completed his search of the greenhouse. Near the back a large pond bubbled and gurgled, tiny fish with colourful tails chasing ripples and dancing shadows. In the middle sat a model of an island that looked strangely familiar. After a few moments, he realised it was Tasmania, but the sea level and coast line were all wrong. Despite this, the other features seemed accurate, including a small model of the compound sitting at the edge of the central plateau and a large river flowing to the south-east. Gibbon made a detailed sketch in his notebook.

Suddenly worried about the goats and his supplies, Gibbon moved the cart inside and swung the large gate closed. He then approached the squat building. The door opened on silent and well-oiled hinges. Inside, dust motes floated through sunlight pouring in from a skylight. Except for a large spiral staircase leading underground, the room was empty. Gibbon stepped inside and cautiously descended into the gloom.

After several revolutions the staircase opened into a long hallway, closed doors scattered along its length. Dim electric lamps, some flickering, were the only illumination. At the end of the hallway was a thick steel door, a small green light shining from above. Gibbon systematically worked up the hallway, finding nothing but dust covered tables, benches and bunks. From behind one door came a deep reverberating hum. It was warm to the touch and had a faded red symbol consisting of three triangles arranged around a circle. Vaguely disturbed, Gibbon left the door closed and backed away.

Gibbon reached the vault door. So far he had found nothing of immediate use. The steel was of course extremely valuable, but he had no tools to cut it out, let alone a way to get it down the mountain. He gripped the wheel with both hands, took a deep breath and spun it. The green light changed to red as the door opened, strange smelling air hissing out. Inside was a small room containing another vault door. To one side hung strange black masks with frayed black hoses. Gibbon tried to open the inner door, but the locking wheel would not yield. It turned only a fraction before a red light flashed insistently and an angry buzzer sounded. Looking again at the masks, he ran his hand around the outer door jamb. Near the latch he found a small mechanism. Pressing on it made a satisfying click and the red light changed to green. With his hand on the switch, Gibbon stretched across the small room and spun the locking wheel. It turned freely and the inner door opened with a hiss of rushing air.

Gibbon stepped forward and peered into the darkness. A small light automatically turned on and began to brighten. He was disappointed as the dark shadows and gloomy shapes resolved into upturned boxes and empty shelves. Gibbon paced the vault, kicking and prodding each box. In the back corner, he kicked one with a particularly virulent level of enthusiasm, yelling in pain as his foot hit something solid. After a moment to regain composure, Gibbon bent down and picked up a small metal box about the size of a suitcase. It was unopened and had an unusual locking mechanism. Not wanting to be trapped in the dark when the flickering lights finally went out, Gibbon did one last check of the vault before returning to the surface.

Sitting next to the brightly coloured fish once more, Gibbon opened the strange metal case. It was difficult to pry open but once slightly ajar, there was a brief burst of inrushing air and it opened freely. Gibbon stared inside at a smaller, glossy white box. The only mark was a silver symbol just like the talisman he had borrowed from Fox. It definitely did look like the outline of an apple with a small bite removed. Inside was a clear piece of rectangular glass about the size and thickness of a periodical. Looking closely, he saw tiny silver and copper coloured tendrils of wire criss-crossing the panel. Also in the box was a cover to hold the panel, the outside of which looked like glossy, stained green leather. The back of the box was covered in strange symbols and a diagram of stick figures storing the panel in the green cover and pointing it at the sun. Gibbon emulated this, placing the glass panel into the cover and putting them both in the sun next to the pond.

After a few moments there was a polite chime. Gibbon opened the case to see the glass panel was now opaque and displaying a column of brightly coloured glyphs, each with text or symbols adjacent. He could almost read one line next to a red glyph with yellow stars, making out the characters for house and language. Gibbon touched it and the screen instantly changed, showing a vista of moving clouds. After a few seconds it filled with rows of glyphs, the clouds still moving peacefully in the background.

Gibbon sat back, holding the reassuring heft of the glass panel in his hand. Back home, several ancient and well respected family dynasties could trace their wealth to a lucky find in an ancient vault. However, to Gibbon's knowledge, nothing of consequence had been uncovered since the great Osaka fire over two hundred years ago. In that unfortunate incident, a professor at Shinano University built an enormous logic engine. Legend had it he needed more than a clipper load of valves! Using this computer and a wireless telegraph he conversed with an ancient, orbiting space capsule, giving commands for it to land on the university lawn. Unfortunately, at a crucial juncture several valves failed and the pod smashed into the warehouse district. The resulting fire razed most of Osaka. No working tek was recovered but the capsules twisted remains are still a popular tourist attraction.

After some thought, Gibbon went and stood beside the two graves. "I humbly accept this mysterious object as full payment for consignment delivery and burial

services." Satisfied that the requirements of social decorum and decency were ful-
filled, Gibbon packed his things along with all the food he could carry. Using the
sketch as a guide, he hiked out of the compound heading due east. Destination, New
Hobart.

Over the next week Gibbon fell into a routine. Days were spent hiking east across
the boulder-strewn and windswept plateau. Meals were a simple affair of nuts, dried
fruit, and cheese. With nothing to burn except the occasional clump of dried grass,
nights were spent shivering in the lee of a boulder. He investigated the glass panel,
trying to uncover more functions. However, most glyphs led only to a picture of a
cloud crossed with a red line. It could, however, acquire marvellously detailed pho-
tographs and Gibbon would often flick idly through his camera gallery, enlarging
the more interesting bushes, rocks and small lakes he had photographed that day.

Assuming the map was accurate and he kept going east, Gibbon was reason-
ably sure he would reach a large river. From there it would be a simple matter of
heading downstream until reaching the first town or village. He hoped so, anyway.
By the second day, after passing another series of unremarkable small lakes, boggy
marshes and non-descript grassy mounds, Gibbon was not sure he could have
found his way back to the compound even if he wanted. And despite being the
middle of summer, nights were biting cold. He doubted this journey was even
possible in any other season. Little wonder that he had seen no Guardians on his
eastward trek; the original builders obviously did not expect many interlopers to
come this way.

On the fifth day the terrain began to gently slope downhill. Gibbon found
himself frequently splashing through tiny streams and the ground was now
firmer. Small trees and shrubs started to appear. On the eighth night he set up
camp next to a fast-flowing creek under a grove of hoop pine trees. Gibbon grate-
fully started a fire and spent the night watching countless sparks float up to join
the stars above.

The next morning Gibbon found a faint trail following the creek downstream.
Several hours of easy hiking bought him to the edge of the plateau. The creek, now
a roaring waterfall, tumbled into the valley below. In the distance, he could see a
collection of buildings next to a large, wide river. Gibbon took out his glass panel
and captured several photos. The marvellous zoom function revealed brightly coloured cottages with roofs covered in dark wooden tiles. Smoke lazily curled up from
several chimneys and he could just make out smudged forms of people loading a
barge tied to a jetty. River traffic meant frequent visitors, so strange travellers
should be welcome. It could even mean the presence of an inn. Stomach grumbling,
Gibbon scampered down into the valley.

Just outside of town Gibbon found a well-used path. Not wanting to encourage unwelcome enquiries, he packed the glass panel carefully in his bag and strolled into the town. The first thing that struck him was how prosperous it seemed. The cobbled roads were bordered by gardens full of perennial herbs, flowers and well-pruned apple trees, branches weighed down heavily with fruit. There was even the occasional electric street lamp. Several locals tending the gardens looked up, smiling and waving as he strolled past. The homes were tidy and comfortable, painted in bright blues, reds and the occasional deep green. To Gibbon's eye they did seem slightly over-built. All were constructed with massive timbers with heavy stone footings. The roof pitch suggested thick snowfall in winter, but perhaps the homes were just built strong against storms. Gibbon continued along the main road between the occasional flock of ducks, their short fluffy tails wagging as they waddled away from the strange visitor.

The road ended at the river banks surrounded by several warehouses filled with logs, dressed timber, large wooden crates and hundreds of barrels and casks. In the distance Gibbon could hear the distinctive whine of a large saw cutting timber. A large two-story building with outdoor seating overlooked the river. A sign depicting a trout jumping a log hung from the entrance. A wooden jetty jutted out into the wide, clear river and tied up alongside was a flat bottomed barge, about sixty to seventy paces long.

A dozen people bustled about, directed by the enthusiastic exclamations of a woman in a green bowler hat. The crew noisily chatted as they hauled on and fussed over ropes, blocks, and tackles. After a few moments the woman noticed Gibbon and walked over. She clasped his hand, shaking vigorously with a hard, calloused grip.

"The name's Kat and I'm the captain of this fine vessel. If you are looking to sail with us downriver I must warn you we run a tight ship with no room for high maintenance or demanding supernumeraries."

Gibbon suppressed a frown, "As a matter of fact I am seeking transportation to New Hobart. I should stress it has often been remarked what an unassuming and undemanding guest I make. Still, one has a few modest requirements which even a vessel of limited means should be able to provide. Firstly, I require a private cabin with a clean bed and wash basin. A full size window would be appreciated, but a porthole will suffice if necessary. Second, a hot breakfast is to be served no earlier than eight. Thirdly I require all linen to be . . ." The glare coming from Kat was such that Gibbon drifted into silence mid-sentence.

"As my vessel is only of limited means, all passengers travel on deck with the freight. A simple meal of stew and bread can be provided for a nominal fee. See you at first light, the charge is ten denarii." With that Kat spun around and marched back down the jetty, only pausing to shout over her shoulder, "You can get lodgings tonight at the Jumping Trout. That is where the other passengers are staying."

Ten denarii seemed excessive but Gibbon thought better of attempting to negotiate. Kat was talking to a small group of her crew, pointing occasionally at him. After a moment they all looked back at Gibbon together and burst out laughing. Red faced, he retreated back across the road and entered the Jumping Trout.

Inside was a spacious room with a dark slate floor adorned by the occasional colourful rug. The ceiling was held aloft by thick wooden beams, each engraved with intricate, swirling patterns. Gibbon noted with approval the well-stocked bar. A wireless at one end was quietly playing a news broadcast. Comfortable couches were arranged alongside bay windows whilst through the back door Gibbon could glimpse the large benches and ovens of a well equipped kitchen. In the centre was a huge hearth, its brick chimney punching through the ceiling above. One man was leaning on the mantle, idly poking red hot coals with a stoking iron. As Gibbon walked through the entrance, a gust of wind caught the door behind him, slamming it shut. The man turned to look at him. After a brief moment of uncomfortable silence he burst out laughing and waved Gibbon to come join him.

He introduced himself as Malvern, manager of the Jumping Trout. Like most publicans he seemed a jovial sort, full of news and gossip, some true, some exaggerated. Gibbon enquired about lodgings and food for the night.

"Not a problem my good friend. However, I must warn you there will be quite the party tonight. As compensation all my guests can partake freely of the bar!"

Gibbon assured him this sounded most suitable.

"I know this isn't my business, but by chance your name is not Fox is it?"

A condensing ball of concern began to form in the pit of Gibbon's stomach as he shook his head.

"Sorry to ask, just that earlier today we got an urgent telegram. Someone by the name of Fox is arriving early tomorrow morning and requested a guide to meet him up at Lamberts Pass to help him down the trail in the dark."

The ball of concern hardened into a lump of outright apprehension. "What would drive someone to be so careless with coin and animal?"

"I don't know, he really wants to be on the barge tomorrow morning I guess. At any rate he is paying good denarii so my daughter Maisie gets to earn some pocket money!"

Gibbon could only guess that Fox must have made it past the Guardians somehow and was now trying to track him down at the first major town east of the compound.

"Yes, very strange. For my own sanity I long ago gave up trying to decipher the madness of others."

"A sensible philosophy," Malvern agreed.

Gibbon paused and took stock for a few moments, staring into the flames and hot coals. "Would it be possible to have someone show me around town? I am new here and seeing the sights would be a capital way to spend the afternoon."

Malvern beamed at the unexpected interest in his town. "I will send Maisie to fetch you once I find her. Don't pay her more than one denarii though, she already rorted five just to walk up and down the north road tonight. Ha-ha!"

Malvern showed Gibbon upstairs to his room, a rather comfortable space with two windows, a solid wooden dresser and a large, soft bed. Malvern chatted on as he fussed with the bed cover and windows. "Hopefully the room is to your satisfaction. It has the best view of the river. The party starts at dusk, don't be late!" And with that he swept out of the room, leaving Gibbon staring through the window watching goods get loaded onto the barge.

Gibbon was still there, pondering stratagems, when Maisie knocked on the door. She was eleven or perhaps twelve years old, wearing sturdy boots, long dark pants, and a vest covered with bulging pockets. Her eyes had an enthusiastic, entrepreneurial glint not yet diminished by age and experience.

"Father says I am to give you the grand tour. He also insisted you get a discount on the normal rate, so it is only five denarii." That she said this with a straight face impressed Gibbon. No doubt she will go far in life, he thought.

"I will of course only pay one denarii, and expect you to run several errands for me during the afternoon."

Intrigued by the opportunities that "running errands" might present, she gave an innocent smile and sped out the door, gesturing impatiently for Gibbon to follow.

The tour confirmed Gibbon's first impression of the town's prosperity. Although Maisie's curt, if not enthusiastic answers often just raised more questions.

"What powers the saw mill and street lights?" Gibbon asked.

"The Hydro-Grid."

"Why are the houses so stout?"

"Else the diprotodons would knock them over."

"Why not hunt or scare the diprotodons away?"

"They stop the devils of course."

"So this town is called Derwent Bridge, no?"

"Yes!"

"So," Gibbon paused for dramatic effect, "where is the bridge?"

Maisie rolled her eyes and gave a look that indicated she thought him perhaps a bit simple.

"Could you run and fetch me a vegetable pasty and flagon of dark ale?"

"Sure, that will cost one denarii," she said, holding out her hand while still walking. Gibbon stopped and just looked at her.

"I mean forty terces," she admitted.

Gibbon smiled. "I will wait here on this convenient bench, it offers a prodigious view of your street gardens." He riffled through his bag, pretending to search for the coins. After a moment Maisie's curiosity overrode her manners and she stepped up on her toes to get a look inside his bag. When her eyes widened Gibbon knew she had glimpsed the shiny talisman that Fox had kindly donated.

"Do you like it?"

Her eyes quickly became disinterested and in a bored tone replied, "It is not completely without merit."

"Well, if you continue to be quick and honest in our dealings you may have it."

"That is kind of you. On an unrelated note, I just remembered there was a recent price change. The food and drink is only thirty terces. Also may I suggest cider rather than the dark ale, it is particularly good this year. So I am told."

Gibbon handed over the coins. "Be quick, my hunger grows with each breath." He waited for her to dart around the corner before sitting on the convenient bench. A family of wrens hopped around his feet chasing insects. The male, with his brilliant blue tail feathers, looked quizzically at Gibbon and found him wanting. He chirped once and the whole family fluttered into a nearby acacia bush.

A few moments later Maisie returned with two pasties, cider and a flavoured milk. As they sat eating lunch Gibbon enquired about any nearby attractions of note.

"Father likes to go fishing in the Great Lakes. He usually takes me along and one time I caught a brown trout longer than my arm!"

"Is it far?"

"Maybe half a day easy walking."

"I have always wanted to catch trout. Such a noble fish, and capital eating. Perhaps I could employ your services to take me there tomorrow? If we leave at dawn we could be fishing by mid-morning?"

Maisie looked down and kicked aimlessly at the ground a few times before explaining she was already busy first thing tomorrow morning to bring in some west coast fool who didn't know it was stupid to travel at night. The trail to the Great Lakes was clear, though, and she could ask Father to draw a simple map for Gibbon to find his way, if he liked. Gibbon made an effort to look suitably disappointed that she couldn't make it. Then he pulled out one of the talismans and handed it to Maisie as his promised payment. She immediately placed the chain over her head and started twisting and turning the silver pendant, looking into the distorted reflections.

"I understand that reflected starlight looks particularly curious," Gibbon suggested.

"Thank you Gibbon, I don't care what the others say. You're not that strange. If you don't need anything else I have to go back home now."

"Thank you Maisie, before you run off is there anyone skilled at leatherwork in town?"

"Old man Williams is, he runs the tannery just behind the mill. Follow your nose!" Maisie enjoyed one last swig on her flavoured milk and scampered down the street, waving goodbye as ducks scattered in her wake.

Later that day Gibbon was in his room watching the remaining goods get loaded onto the barge, the river reflecting the dull orange glow of a cloudy sunset. His errands had gone well, the results of which were now in his bag and a small wooden barrel sitting on the jetty. A crewman moved his barrel onto the barge, stacking it neatly with the other freight near the bow. A heavy canvas sail was then placed over them like a blanket and tied down within a web of ropes. Satisfied his goods were secure, Gibbon turned to leave the room. The party had already started and he intended to test the extent of Malvern's food and drink-inclusion policy. Gibbon descended the stairs into loud music, mouth-watering smells from the kitchen, and dozens of brightly-dressed, smiling revellers.

A rooster crowing. Lapping water. Creaking ropes. Where am I? Gibbon thought. He rolled off a stack of sail cloth onto wooden planking. The barge—he had gone to sleep on the barge. A high voice drifted across the water. Head throbbing, Gibbon sat up slowly and wiped his eyes. The only light was from a single street lamp in front of the Jumping Trout. Underneath it stood Maisie, enthusiastically explaining something to a tired looking man sitting on a horse. The silver talisman was clearly visible around her neck. Gibbon groaned as he recognised the round face and short stature of Fox. Garbled memories of telling everyone he was off fishing before hiding on the barge now made more sense. Maisie continued her exuberant elucidations, pausing for Fox's acknowledgement at the more important junctures. After a few moments Malvern stepped outside and Maisie fell silent. He said something to Fox which Gibbon couldn't make out and then handed over a small piece of paper. Fox asked something and Malvern replied by pointing towards the brightening eastern sky. Fox seemed satisfied and handed over several coins to Maisie. A few clicks of encouragement and his horse reluctantly turned and started towards the Great Lakes. Maisie waved until he rounded a corner and then turned to her father and excitedly showed him the various coins and trinkets she had acquired over the past few days. Malvern listened patiently, smiling as they walked back inside the Jumping Trout. Gibbon wedged himself between two crates and fell asleep using his bag as a lumpy pillow.

"Cat, I found another one."

Gibbon staggered upright, squinting eyes trying to make out his surroundings. The barge was underway, Derwent Bridge fading into the distance and a bright sun poking above the trees. Passengers and crew milled about the deck. Some of them looked worse than he felt.

"My word it's bright."

The crewman who found him just laughed and yelled again. "It's that posh man who thinks we run a Blue Moon clipper!"

From the back of the barge Cat replied, still yelling, "Standard fare."

"Stowaways pay extra. Twenty denarii, please."

Gibbon responded by violently and repeatedly vomiting over the side.

The barge smoothly floated downstream. Occasionally, in places where the river widened, crew would man poles or sweeps to keep the speed up. Gradually the tall trees and dark timber morphed into rolling green hills covered in a patchwork of stone fences and the occasional small village. At one point two entrepreneurs rowed out and did a brief roaring trade selling steaming hot pies. The sun climbed higher into the blue sky; it was shaping up to be a hot day. Cat ordered a sail to be placed up as an awning and most of the passengers settled under it in idle conservation.

There were a dozen of them, including Gibbon. Many felt the need to expand endlessly on their various life stories, much to Gibbon's annoyance. The most loquacious were a recently married young couple moving from Derwent Bridge to New Hobart. The town co-operative had pooled funds to buy them into an apprenticeship with a prestigious furniture maker. This, they tediously explained, was a great way to keep Derwent Bridge's population stable and avoid a crushing Malthus tax bill. Eventually, they would move back with new skills and Derwent Bridge could add additional value to the timber it harvested.

A group of five men and women, all wearing heavy blue robes, nodded in agreement. They had just spent the past two years visiting countries all around the Pacific Rim. They noted with disapproval that some nations did not employ any type of Malthus taxes, preferring instead to levy the product of labour. Did these people not study any history they wondered?

Another passenger, a woman who introduced herself as Jenner, had spent the past week collecting hydrographic readings for Hydro-Grid head office. She posited that those states not lucky enough to have an ancient working Hydro-Grid might draw comfort from a rapidly growing population and the additional labour it provides.

One of the blue robes could not agree. "Surely they know that by definition a growing population must eventually extinguish their resources and fall into conflict with neighbours?"

Jenner nodded and went on. "Perhaps they feel entitled to some of those resources. It can be easy to forget, well-fed and floating blissfully down this bountiful land, that many in the world don't have electricity to do work for them, or a grand steel hulled wind jammer fleet to protect trade routes and borders."

"What do you suggest instead? If we shared what we had with the world, everyone would be equally poor. I don't see any advantage in that scenario."

A nearby crew member added, "It is a moot point anyway. The Hydro-Grid is solid and immovable. We can't simply give it to others. Besides, our manufactured goods are openly traded for fair prices. In this way the whole world benefits from our productivity."

Many nodded in agreement to this sensible statement of fact.

Another passenger added, "In ancient times governments used to dominate entire continents and they just made things worse. Perhaps the answer lies at an individual rather than national level?"

Murmurs rippled around the group, people now unsure how responsible they should feel.

Jenner turned to face Gibbon. "What do you think? Should we strive to share all we produce equally with the world?"

The group looked expectantly at Gibbon, his prior policy of silence already adding weight to his words. "In a purely theoretical sense I completely agree. Poverty is a distressing condition that no one should experience. It is at the practical day to day level that my well-meaning intentions struggle to find expression."

One of the blue-robes was now philosophically adrift, asking, "Are you suggesting nothing should be done about the world's injustice?"

"I used to work with a mentat who claimed the universe floated on a quantum foam of infinite possibilities. If he is right, there must be a version of me somewhere that has done the right thing, whatever that may be. Surely this is enough?"

Gibbon noted with satisfaction the confused looks as everyone fell silent and returned to watching the countryside glide past.

As the river widened the towns got bigger and traffic increased. Small dinghies cast nets in the shallows. A barge steamed upstream, it's small charcoal powered motor struggling against the current. Another was towed by oxen trudging along the grassy banks. A favourable breeze blew in from the west and Cat ordered the lateen sail raised. The barge heeled ever so slightly as it picked up speed, now going faster than the river current. Gibbon watched pleasure craft cross their gurgling wake.

Not long after lunch (fried fish and potato chips delivered by a family in a long canoe) Gibbon could taste salt in the air. By mid-afternoon pacific gulls lazily circled high above. The river widened further and Cat announced they would be soon arriving. The barge, surrounded by boats of all shapes and sizes, colourful sails fluttering, tacked around a rocky finger of land. Above them in the cliffs, there was a massive, sprawling and rust coloured building cut into the side, dominating the approach.

"The Museum of New and Old," Jenner remarked to no one in particular. "They say it has enough steel to build two windjammers, but even during the Maori wars a century ago, they ripped up the railways first. It is the oldest building in New Hobart, constructed to protect knowledge and treasures as the oceans rose. Must be at least five hundred years old . . ."

The group stared in silent awe as they floated by a wonder of the ancient world. They were quickly distracted however as Derwent Bay opened up before them.

New Hobart. Homes, workshops, church towers, observatories and government buildings all nestled under the towering bulk of Mt Wellington, its peak wreathed in cloud. The occasional tall radio mast betrayed the presence of a wireless station or telegraph office. Closer to the shore were factories, warehouses and hotels. Among them all were a myriad of people on foot, horseback and buggy. An electric trolley glided along the waterfront promenade, stopping occasionally for passengers to get on or off. The harbour was just as busy. A steam tug gently guided a New England clipper towards the quay. Alongside bobbed cogs from Maori bulging with the finest wool, fast cats from Solomon with tropical fruits and storm lashed fishing boats from Antarctica. Amongst them a myriad of small craft darted back and forth. Overlooking them all, an enormous four-masted steel windjammer riding at easy anchor, pennants flapping in the breeze, long guns glinting in the sunlight. Bigger, stronger and faster than any wooden clipper, one salvo from its long guns could smash even the thickest oak. They, along with the hydro-grid powered arc furnaces needed to build them, were the only reason such a small island could dominate the entire Pacific Rim.

Cat and her crew expertly threaded the barge through harbour traffic and glided into an empty berth. Young boys on the wharf ran up to take lines and tie them off. Gibbon thought he caught a particularly ugly one staring. A gangplank dropped into place and the passengers dawdled onto the wharf. Cat announced their goods would be ready to collect from the warehouse after dinner and suggested the Steel Windlass for an excellent house stew while they wait. Those who travelled light, including Jenner, disappeared into the milling crowd. Gibbon followed the remaining passengers across the road and into the tavern.

The passengers huddled around the bar, reflecting on their journey and the relative merits of various cities. Gibbon detected a tedious tone of self-congratulation sneaking into the conversation and moved to sit alone in a booth by the window. Coin pouch on his belt and bag at his feet, Gibbon enjoyed a hearty stew served in crusty trenchers whilst watching Cat and her crew begin unloading.

Several tankards of dark ale later, Gibbon noted with satisfaction his barrel loaded onto a trolley and pushed into a nearby warehouse. He moved to get up but a rough hand grabbed his shoulder, pushing him back into the booth.

"In a hurry, Mr. Gibbon sir?"

Gibbon stared in disbelief at the rotund man who slid into the seat opposite. The oaf attached to the rough hand sat next to Gibbon, squashing him against the window. The ugly boy, still staring at Gibbon, waited by the table.

"Mr Fox. What a pleasant and, I must say, unexpected surprise. I thought you would be enjoying the Great Lakes by now."

Fox continued to smile as he handed a coin to the boy, who immediately ran off without a word of thanks. "Yes, well that was a rather clever ruse, wasn't it? It took me a few hours to realise it seemed out of character for you to just give the talisman to that annoying girl."

"I am sure if you want it back she will sell it to you. Feel free to mention my name, you might get a discount," Gibbon offered.

"Don't be coy Gibbon. I know the old man is dead. Whatever you stole from him rightly belongs to me."

"I couldn't possibly know what you mean Fox. I delivered the goods, took payment and moved on. Here, I can give you half now if you like." Gibbon reached inside his jacket but stopped at a threatening grunt from the oaf.

Fox nodded and the oaf reached under the table, grabbed Gibbon's bag and upended it, contents spilling onto the table.

"Please be careful with those." Gibbon's plea fell on deaf ears as the oaf and Fox greedily rummaged through the pile. An expensive spiral bound notebook, pencils, a jet black feather, jaunty red cap, a threadbare towel and a small locket of brown hair tied in a purple ribbon all flung carelessly aside.

Fox picked up a thin coat and opened it to reveal the deep green cover Gibbon found with the glass panel.

"Ahh, what do we have here?"

Gibbon groaned. The oaf grunted.

Fox opened the cover before glaring at Gibbon as he threw it back down on the table. A laminated wooden board with "Greetings from Derwent Bridge" engraved into one side bounced out and slid across the table.

Fox's jovial face had transformed into an animal snarl, a small line of dribble forming in the corner of his mouth.

"You think to trick me Gibbon? Do you know how long I made those tedious deliveries to the old man? He was hiding something, something ancient and doubtless valuable. I want it!" Nearby patrons began to glance nervously at the table. Gibbon remained silent, picking up the cover and wooden board, carefully placing them back in his bag along with his other possessions. The oaf pointed through the window at the barge and grunted. Fox paused to look at several crates coming off the barge and stood up.

"Let's go, we have a warehouse to check."

The oaf opened his jacket just wide enough for Gibbon to see the enormous knife tucked in his belt before grabbing him in a vice grip and following Fox outside.

It was late afternoon, the heat of the day still radiating from the stone buildings and cobbled road. The streets were busy, but no one paid any heed as Fox and his minion guided Gibbon towards the nearby warehouse. They approached the entrance where one of Cat's crew stood with a ledger, co-signing deliveries and pickups.

"Try to warn anyone and they will be the first to die," Fox warned. The oaf grunted an enthusiastic agreement.

The crewmen looked up, smiling. "Uh, ahh, good afternoon Gibbon. I hope you found the boat's amenities met your exacting standards. We do hate to leave our guests unsatisfied." He was struggling to hold back laughter. Clearly this was the height of humour.

Gibbon took a deep breath, ready to go through his carefully compiled list of sensible improvements before the oaf jammed his knife handle painfully between Gibbon's ribs.

"Never mind that, I just came for my barrel," Gibbon snapped.

The crewman dropped his smile and pointed through the open door. "Out back with the others, don't leave without signing the consignment sheet on your way out."

Gibbon nodded as he untangled himself from the oaf's grip and led the way into the warehouse.

Crates, hessian bags and wooden barrels were haphazardly stacked everywhere, many with foreign symbols and exotic names stamped on the side. After a few wrong turns Gibbon found the Derwent Bridge consignment in a quiet corner below a weak electric lamp. Trying to stall for time, Gibbon made conservation.

"What do you think the old man was hiding, Fox? Weapons? Fantastic energy sources? Maybe electrically stimulated hallucinations?"

"Does it matter, Gibbon? Someone would have paid good denarii. Isn't that all that counts?" His face relaxing back to its natural jovial state, Fox continued, "No doubt you had much grander and noble plans?"

Gibbon found his barrel and rolled it back into the light. "I suppose in a relative sense, any benefits from this hypothetical treasure would be noble to my own person. That much at least is clear to me."

Fox just shook his head and directed for Gibbon to open the barrel. After much straining Gibbon pried away the cover and stood back. The oaf leant over to have a look but Fox pushed him out of the way and stared into a barrel packed tightly with smoked trout. Fox sighed and nodded at the oaf who began indiscriminately flinging out whole fish onto the warehouse floor.

"What do you think you're doing? That is the finest smoked fish you can get this side of the Pacific Rim!"

Fox and Gibbon looked up to see Jenner standing just outside the circle of light. Gibbon, noticing her expression was more "disinterested quoll playing with its food" than "concerned citizen witnessing a crime," took a step back. The oaf, not one for picking up subtle social cues, dropped a piece of smoked trout back into the barrel, pulled out his knife and moved towards Jenner. He didn't make it two steps. There was a high pitched whine followed by an explosion of blue sparks on his chest. The oaf slumped onto the ground, his foot twitching. Two uniformed guards moved out of the gloom, one of them holding a short rifle covered in brass tubes connected to a large backpack. A faint tinge of ozone lingered in the air. Fox turned to run but two more officers moved to block him, both holding large batons. Fox stopped, carefully straightened his clothes and turned back to face Jenner. "Provocateur Max, I can't say it is a pleasure to see you again."

"I was eager to catch up, you left in such a hurry last time." Max nodded and two officers stepped forward, tied Fox's hands, and escorted him from the building.

"So I suppose you don't really work for the Hydro-Grid, do you, Max? Or is it Jenner?" Gibbon queried.

"You can call me Max if you wish. The bigger question is what you have got hidden in that barrel that dragged Fox away from his smuggler friends in the Western Isles?"

Gibbon, knowing when to quit, smiled. "Perhaps he just wanted some capital smoked trout?"

"I will be sure to send some to his cell. Now, if you could be so kind as to empty that barrel."

Gibbon stepped over the oaf and upended the barrel, a square leather bag falling from the bottom. A baton wielding officer grabbed the bag and opened it, pulling out the dark green cover.

"It looks like some sort of book with a stained leather binding ma'am."

Max took the "book" and opened it, revealing the translucent glass panel within.

"It is a little more advanced than a book." Max touched the glass panel, which powered on, displaying a close up picture of Gibbon's face. "Although it remains to be seen if it is any more useful."

"Some of those photos are private," insisted Gibbon.

"Yes, I see," Max agreed, as she scrolled through some of the gallery items. "Check his bag. Make sure he isn't hiding anything else."

The guard quickly and carefully checked everything in Gibbon's bag. "Nothing of interest except three hundred denarii and a wooden copy of that thing you have there." He passed the wooden "glass panel" in its dark green cover to Max.

"Well, it is lovely workmanship, Gibbon, but I am not sure it would have fooled anyone. You do realise the penalties for concealing ancient tek are . . . severe."

Gibbon swallowed. "I of course had every intention to notify the relevant authorities." Taking a gamble, Gibbon continued, "Perhaps we could go begin that process now. I imagine there would be a lot of people interested in seeing an ancient marvel such as this."

Max frowned. "You are overplaying a precarious position, Gibbon. Still, all things considered, you have delivered me a useful item. Providing the opportunity to reward Fox for his many and varied crimes is icing on the cake." Pausing to place the wooden "glass panel" and its cover back in Gibbon's bag, she went on. "The tide will be ebbing in less than an hour. The Harvest Moon clipper Wanderlust will be departing on it. Make sure you are on board."

Gibbon picked up his bag and stared regretfully at the trout scattered around the oaf's body.

"Am I to expect no recompense for my damaged goods?"

Max scowled and turned to her guards. "Escort our friend to the docks."

"Yes ma'am."

Officers on the quarterdeck tipped their hats in acknowledgement as the steam tug gave a shrill whistle and turned back into the harbour. With so many mariners watching from the harbour it wouldn't do to have the jib or mizzen billowing about in a lubberly and un-seaman-like manner, but the crew did their ship credit, studding sails and topgallants falling simultaneously from all four masts. The Wanderlust began to heel in the gentle nor-wester, making a respectable eight knots out of Derwent Bay and into the Southern Ocean.

Sitting on his private balcony overlooking the ship's wake, Gibbon watched New Hobart recede under a setting sun. A discreet knock announced the arrival of his personal steward, who placed a tray of vintage Flinders red wine and a selection of fine cheeses, crackers and dried fruit on the table. Waving the steward away, Gibbon smiled to himself. All things considered, the day had gone well. Losing the glass panel was unfortunate but not unexpected. And though novel, without a "cloud," it was essentially useless. Meanwhile, the real treasure remained his and, if natural justice prevailed, would no doubt deliver a favourable outcome. The Wanderlust began a gentle rolling motion as it entered open water. Confident in his future good fortune, a smiling Gibbon raised his glass towards Mt Wellington, silhouetted against a red sky.

It wasn't till the early hours of the morning when Max was able to sit back at her desk with a whiskey. Her windowless office deep beneath The Museum of New and Old had no windows overlooking the harbour, but her men had reported back when the Wanderlust departed, Gibbon confirmed on board. Max smiled to herself. Apparently Gibbon was not impressed that the only ticket left for the two week journey to Shinano cost 280 denarii. It might have been prudent to eliminate him, but another body would have raised questions. This way her team had exclusive access to the glass panel and any lucrative secrets it contained. In time she would inform her superiors of the find. Max took a sip of whiskey as Jacek from the laboratory poked his head around the corner.

"The device's battery is flat, ma'am, so I sent the team home for the night. Tomorrow we can rig up a charger and begin the detailed analysis."

"That's fine, Jacek. Did Fox give us the location of the compound?"

"Not yet, but our friend was an avid photographer. I think we should be able to identify landmarks in each photo and work back from Derwent Bridge."

"Good work. Now go home to Neve, Jacek. Once that charger is working there will be many long nights ahead of us."

Jacek nodded as he retreated from the doorway. Max took another sip and tried to relax but a nagging thought floated just of reach, something about all those photos they had found. She shouted through the open doorway.

"Jacek, you still there?"

The sound of soft-soled shoes sliding on stone presaged his return.

"Yes ma'am?"

"Tell me, how does someone crossing the highlands for over a week keep a portable computer fully charged?"

Jacek leaned forward slightly, his face a pained expression as he slowly realised the only possible way Gibbon could have kept it charged.

"He must have got a charger from the same place he got the glass panel."

Max nodded in agreement.

Jacek, thinking aloud, continued, "But all you found in his bag was that wooden copy in a green leather case?"

"Well, the case the glass panel came in was leather. On reflection the other case looked a little different . . ." Max paused, recollecting some of the solar cell fragments stored upstairs. The expression on Jacek's face said he had also remembered that obscure exhibit.

Max cursed under her breath. She was never a fan of the cramped windjammer cabins. Still, at least Shinano was nice this time of year.

A Light
in the Forest
by Al Sevcik

ZANE'S LEFT HAND GRIPPED THE REINS OF A LIMPING HORSE and his right probed the path with a stick, a weathered, cloth-covered bundle strapped to his back. He stopped to contemplate the sun, already on it's nightly descent to the horizon. Between him and the sun, as far as he could see, lay the Tampa Wetlands—a grassy expanse of soft earth and treacherous muck-holes crossed by unpredictable trails. Two days behind him now, the wetlands eased into an undefined area of progressively deeper and saltier water called Tampa Bay. Looking a half mile ahead, he saw the trail disappear into dark growth, bushes guarding the forest's edge, followed by trees.

His fingers brushed black hair off his forehead, then tested the two-day growth on his cheeks. *I would have been far into the forest before dark,* he thought, *if things had gone as I planned.* The trek yesterday had been routine. The old mare had done her job. She had carried him on a tenuous path from the coast, testing each step before applying her full weight. But bad luck had come with the morning: a false trail, his horse sensing quicksand a second too late, and now with a wretched limp. *Hopefully it's just a sprain.* He tried to push back the worry. *It will be days before I can ride her again.*

As the shadows lengthened, a bird, black with white striped wings, glided across the trail ahead and hovered over a nearby pond before descending to the water in slow circles. Its soft and silent landing caused gently spreading rings. The bird rested a moment, then frantically flapped its wings and shrieked, spraying water as it was pulled beneath the surface. The bird's cry ricocheted through his mind as Zane watched the pool's surface settle to its previous calm. He stepped back from the water's edge.

It may be safer in the forest. I better keep moving before the daylight goes. He felt the land slope upward as he continued his careful probing of the trail. When he reached the trees, he stopped. *At last! Actual, dry, dirt.* The trail continued into the trees, but the world had become dark. *Now, where do I go?* The one place on earth that he knew, the fishing village of Conroe, Texas was unthinkably far away. A local story was that the town had once been far inland from Houston City. Now it edged the Bay where ragged tops of buildings reached into the air when winter wind pushed water out into the Gulf. The rest of the time the concrete spires and metal beams rested below the surface, snagging unwary watercraft.

A brief meeting, two cold sentences, and his world had been upended. He couldn't remain in Conroe. He had tacked and jibbed his way along the southern edge of the continent until forced by threat of a summer hurricane into Tampa Bay on the swamp coast of old Florida. Oak-colored fisher-people, the result of a two-hundred year blending of genes and cultures, helped pull his boat safely onto shore, their eyes brimming with questions that they were too polite to ask. His boat was combined with the village's fishing fleet and tied with inch-thick rope to a giant anchor buried in the sand.

Zane spent the night with the community's four dozen residents in a cabin made of logs that an earlier generation had wrestled from far away Florida highlands. The wind's increasing strength made the group uneasy, but when that appeared to be the worst of the storm, everyone relaxed. As the buzz of conversation died, eyes turned to Zane. He looked around at the men with calloused hands, at their wives and families. He said, "I grew up in a town in Texas. There's a girl there I've known for a long time. Long-time friends, you know, kids together." His voice grew louder and his grip on the chair's back whitened his knuckles. "That's not true. She and I, we're much more than friends. She can't just turn her back . . ." He stopped and inhaled. His voice softened. "That's what I thought. I assumed . . . well, it turns out that's not the way things really are."

Heads nodded and there were sympathetic sounds. A white-haired, bent over man said, "It's a common enough story."

Zane went on. "A guy from a coastal sloop said he knew where I should go. He said he heard about a place called Orlando, in Florida. He said it might be in the old Florida highlands. That sounds good to me, it's a long ways from Texas. That's what I want. I'm going to find Orlando and start my life again. Can anyone tell me the way?"

They all turned to look at the white haired man. His voice was soft. "Many years ago I met a man older than I am now who talked about Orlando and an old kingdom. He talked about mysterious things and about a castle, but he had an unsure memory." He looked around the room. "We have all known people, strangers, to go from here. They said they were going to follow trails across the swamps to a forest on hills beyond. In my lifetime no one has come the other way. Childhood stories say that the creatures of swamp and forest are not always what they seem." He looked hard at Zane. "That's all I will say."

In the morning there was the expected haggling. Zane thought he did okay. The sailboat wasn't all that great so an old mare, a much-used saddle, and a backpack full of dry food seemed a fair trade.

Now, as stars appeared he stood between swamp and forest wondering what to do. His mind replayed the shriek of the bird as it was pulled under. He turned to look back and glimpsed a shadow moving across the trail and into a water hole. Or maybe there hadn't been a shadow or maybe it hadn't moved. He decided to go into the forest.

His let his eyes adjust to the forest dark. Tree tops shifted against the sky-glow, allowing hints of starlight to trace the forest trail. On either side trees and shadows receded into a deeper darkness. Zane's mare jerked her head back. He stroked her neck. "Come on, girl. They're only shadows. No cause to be frightened." Holding the reins, he moved into the forest, his senses alert.

A firefly floated among the trees. *First one of those I've seen since Texas.* He squinted to focus his eyes. The light didn't move. He stepped to the side. The light flickered. *Ah, it's behind trees and brush.* Guiding a reluctant horse he half-walked, half-felt his way along the uneven path towards the light. When leafy tendrils brushed his arm he shifted a few inches the other way. As he stepped around dense brush the light came into clear view a hundred feet ahead. A square log cabin about eight feet on each side stood by the side of the trail. The light was from a wide open door. Zane turned around and led his horse back along the trail for a quarter mile. He undid the bridle and slid the saddle off. He tied the horse to brush. Then he went back. Near to the cabin he stepped behind a tree. He called, "Hello." No response. Again, "Hello."

Staying in the brush he moved with slow steps nearer to the structure, then threw a stick that struck the wall with a soft thud. There was the crack of a breaking branch in the blackness beyond nearby trees. Zane froze, holding his breath. After a minute he relaxed and again studied the building. *It looks like a guard house, but what's it doing here?* By slow steps he went to the door and looked inside. He saw a rough wood table, oil lamp, and a wood bench with wide feet at either end. He stepped inside, picked up the lamp and shook it. *Feels almost full. Might be enough to last 'til morning.* He closed the cabin door and sat on the floor with his back against the wall. He thought, *I've got two choices, the forest or the cabin. The cabin seems best.*

Something sharp pressed against his throat. His eyes snapped open, his body still. The woman holding the spear eased it back, but steadied it a quarter inch from his skin. "No one from around here would fall asleep in a strange cabin." She was easily six feet tall, almost as tall as Zane. Her iridescent green eyes studied his face. Red-blond hair was gathered into a waterfall that fell halfway down her back. Arm muscles grew and relaxed with her movements. The hand that wasn't holding the spear cradled a rifle; a skinning knife hung at her side. A faded green shirt hung loose over trousers of dark home-spun cloth sprinkled with unexpected colored threads.

He said, "May I sit up?"

"No. Not yet." Reaching with one foot, she dragged the bench close and sat down while the point of the spear rested on Zane's collar bone. "I've had all sorts of odd critters attracted to this light at night, or to one of my traps, but this is the first time I've caught something like you." She pulled the spear point back a little. "What are you? First off, are you real?"

Zane inched his back up against the wall as she adjusted the spear. "I'm real enough. Who are you?"

"I'm still doing the asking, and tuck your hands behind your back." She waited for him to reposition himself, then studied him for several seconds. She said, "Why?"

He looked up at her. "Why anything? I suppose you're asking why I'm here at the wrong end of your spear."

"That would be a good place to start."

"Up 'til now I've spent my life in Texas, on the coast, the edge of Houston Bay." She looked at him with a blank expression.

"If you're sailing in a fishing dingy it's eight days from here."

She nodded.

"I had to leave. Someone said I would find what I wanted in Florida." He noticed a millimeter lifting of her right eyebrow. He said, "I know. Sometimes people don't know what they are talking about, but I was finished with Texas anyway. I sailed along the coast until I had to wait out a storm at Tampa Bay. Folks there told me to come this way. Left Tampa Bay two days ago; my mare lamed her leg yesterday. Been walking from sunup today." He shrugged. "And I'm here."

She stared at him, her eyes wide.

"What?"

"You have a horse?"

"Yes. My mare is tied to a bush about a quarter mile back on the trail."

"I came the other way, so I didn't know." She sighed, her lips compressed, then pulled the spear back and leaned it against the wall. "The horse is . . . You don't have a horse any more."

He came to his knees, moving to stand. "What? I'm going to check—"

She raised her arm to block him. "I grew up in and out of the forest. I know this place. I know for certain that by the time you take fifty steps beyond the light from this lamp you will be dead. Having died unpleasantly." His eyes moved to her rifle. "That won't work. Here a rifle, spear, knife can be used in the light. But they're no use in the dark."

They sat silently looking at each other. She stood and stretched. "Your name?"

"Zane."

"I'm called Tawna. It's six hours to the next sun and I'm going to spend that time sleeping." She kicked the door closed then shrugged off a small backpack and extracted a leather jacket, which she folded and placed on the floor. She set her rifle beside her and lay down with her head on the jacket and closed her eyes. "The lamp stays lit. Go outside to pee but keep the door open and stay in the light. If you step away from the cabin it's likely you won't come back. Nothing out there is your friend. We'll probably be okay in here with the door closed."

"Probably?"

There wasn't any response and in a few minutes her breathing became deep and regular. Zane sat with his back against the log wall. He fingered the straw-reinforced mud daub plastered over the narrow spaces between the logs. From the other side, the dark side of the wall, there was the rustling of foliage, the occasional crack of a breaking stick, a bird's sleepy call, insect buzz, and unidentifiable noises. He pushed away from the wall and lay with his back on the floor and closed his eyes.

Tawna rose with the sun. Zane watched her stretch, kneel on the floor to repack her jacket, then grab her rifle and release the safety. She stood and cracked open the door. With total concentration, she slowly pulled the door back until the forest and the soft light of sunrise filled the opening. She went out, stepped to a bush, and started to push down her trousers. Zane turned his head to the wall until her footsteps sounded on the cabin floor. He felt a soft kick against his back.

"Your turn. Do your stuff and then we'll find some breakfast."

He grunted, rolled over, stood and stepped out onto dew-wet grass. After relieving himself, he surveyed the cabin and the forest. Time paused, the world held its breath, no leaf moved. He had the sense of standing in a fake tableau, one with too many shades of green. Around him flowers materialized from foliage hiding places. He looked down and his neck hairs lifted. Padded paws had pushed four large prints into the soft earth. The kind of paws with retractable claws. He went back inside.

"You saw the prints."

He nodded.

"I've never seen the critter and I don't want to." She shouldered her pack and turned off the lamp. "Let's go." After closing the door she began a fast walk, retracing the way he had come yesterday.

He said, "You took a risk last night. Going to sleep. Leaving me free."

She stopped. "I don't take risks. Your brain may have been slow to catch on, but your subconscious knew not to touch me. My help is essential if you want to get out of the forest. Think about it. Last night you were my prisoner. You still are." Turning her back, she continued walking.

Zane followed silently. *Thinks she controls the world*. He shrugged. *I'll let her be in charge—for awhile*.

Tawna stopped to study the foliage. She pushed branches aside and left the trail. Zane followed her through the brush for a hundred feet. "There," she said. "There's your horse." She nodded to a circle of broken branches, bones and blood. "Not enough meat scraps to save. Your saddle looks okay. Pick it up, we don't have far to go."

Swallowing hard, Zane lifted reins and bit from bloody grass. Holding these and the saddle under one arm, he followed Tawna further into brush until the undergrowth thinned and they walked on leaf covered ground beneath the tree canopy. Tawna stopped and whistled, four distinct notes. She repeated the whistle again. "I'm calling Aeon, my horse."

Zane dropped the reins and saddle. "Your horse? You left your horse here all night, but my mare . . ."

Brushing leaves aside, Tawna dragged a blanket of woven reeds from under a bush. She removed other leaves from canvas bags attached at the ends of a cloth belt that would fit a horse. She then looked around until she found a flat rock and sat, knees up, ankles crossed. "Aeon is from the forest. He was born here; it's in his blood. I learn as best I can, but Aeon just knows. He's knows the most important thing: how to survive." She stood. "He's here."

As Zane watched, a shadow disconnected from the trees and became a horse. A black stallion with wide hooves, powerful legs and muscles that rippled across his chest as he walked towards them. The horse stopped, brown eyes studying Zane. Tawna spoke. "It's all right, Aeon." She went to the horse and rubbed her hand in repeated circles on his neck while she spoke in a low voice. After a minute Aeon raised his head, shook his mane, and followed Tawna. "He's willing to take both of us." She placed the blanket across the horse's back. "I'll mount first. Stuff your saddle into one of the bags and get on. We'll use that stump for a step."

They rode in silence until Tawna reached forward and touched Aeon's neck. The horse stepped off the path and stopped beside a pile of rock. Tawna slid to the ground. Zane followed and then saw that the rocks were piled at the end of a lichen-covered wall that disappeared into foliage a short distance away.

Eying the rocks and the wall, Tawna said, "They've done some repairs."

Zane frowned. "They?"

Turning to the bags she had strapped to her horse, Tawna produced a coarsely woven sack. She motioned with her hand. "Come." Zane followed her along the edge of the wall where the grass was worn. They avoided stems with thorns and occasional three-leaved branches that looked to Zane like Texas poison ivy. "Because of all the thrashing about when your mare was killed last night I knew there wouldn't be any game in my traps by the cabin. So we came here first." She lifted her hand. "Wait." She disappeared into the foliage. In minutes she returned holding the ears of a brown rabbit. The rabbit struggled for release until Tawna slammed a fist-sized rock against its skull. She popped the carcass into a bag and looked at Zane. "This is one of the things I do for the community. I persuade the forest to provide us with meat."

Handing Zane the sack, she continued along the wall. She spoke into the air. "Of course we have cattle and pigs. Forest food is special." At the next trap she showed Zane how to reset the bamboo spring and position a sharpened bamboo needle.

The day warmed as the sun worked its way through leaves and high branches.

Tawna lead him to a dozen traps, half of them holding game, then she nodded towards a grassy gully ahead. "Down there." Shortly they were kneeling beside a clear stream. Tawna rubbed her hands in the water then cupped them for a drink. After that she opened the bag and dumped furry bodies onto the grass. She unsheathed her knife, cut off a rabbit's head and slit its body open. She passed the bloody body to Zane. "Scrape it and wash. We'll gut these now and skin them later."

"Tawna, down!" Zane hurled himself against her and they both crumpled into the grass as a spear-headed bird, a projectile with yard-wide wings, flashed over them so close they felt the push of air. Hands shaking, Zane sat back on his knees. Tawna pushed up on her elbows. Their eyes met with a psychic jolt—a momentary exposure of human vulnerability as each struggled to recover from fright. Her face recomposed. Zane looked down trying to calm his mind, still vibrating from the incandescent moment when each had seen a truth about the other.

Standing, she slapped at her clothing and spoke brusquely. "I've never seen those birds so aggressive. Maybe it wanted one of our rabbits. Doesn't matter. We've got lots more work to do." Pulling wood shavings and flint from her pocket she quickly breathed sparks into a fire, then added sticks. She took a cleaned rabbit from Zane, cut off it's paws and then removed the brown fur. She cut the body in half lengthwise and supported each half on sticks close to the fire. She said, "One for brunch, one for dinner; berries in between."

After eating they hiked back to the beginning of the stone wall and waited for Aeon to materialize from sun speckled shadows. To mount the horse, Zane jumped up onto the wall. He studied how the stones fit tight together. "What did you mean when you said 'they' repaired the wall? Who?"

"I don't know. Sometimes in the forest things happen that . . ." She kicked a stone. "Get on. Let's go."

As the afternoon progressed, the two bags strapped to Aeon's sides filled with eviscerated rabbits and other small game. Riding behind Tawna, Zane had to position his legs around the bulging bags with increasing discomfort. He was about to say something when Tawna turned Aeon into the trailside brush. If there was a path it was invisible to Zane. Tawna slid her fingers across the horse's neck to guide it through bushes and then on a vine covered forest floor for about a mile. The ground sloped up as they stepped out of the trees into a grass and flower glade a hundred feet across. A little higher at the center of the glade stood crumbling ruins of concrete, steel and brick. Pieces of the old structure spiked up twenty feet like bony fingers scratching the sky.

When Aeon stopped beside the cracked concrete foundation Tawna slid to the ground. Zane opened his mouth but Tawna interrupted, "Don't bother to ask. Who knows what this is? Two or three centuries ago it may have been important." Together they unfastened the cinch around the horse and eased the sacks of game onto concrete. Tawna pulled the reed blanket off Aeon's back, gathered it in her arms and gave the horse's rump three pats. Aeon stepped away to put his nose into grass.

Tawna said, "Welcome to the best hotel in the forest. Open space between us and the trees and some shelter from rain." She glanced at the sky, now a fading pink. "But I don't think rain's going to happen." She carried the horse blanket across the concrete and spread it under a questionable overhang. "This is my secret place, so no fire tonight. Cold roast rabbit for dinner. But first, a short walk to water." She shrugged off her knapsack, reached in and pulled out a waxed canvas bag. "This will do. Let's go."

Light faded to gloom when they re-entered the forest. She grabbed his arm. "Zane, stop. Don't move."

At first nothing, then his brain saw it; four feet of green on a darker green branch, motionless except for its head, turned to him, swaying from side to side. Translucent blue eyes halved by vertical black slits regarded Zane with . . . hostility? Curiosity? Indifference? Whatever it was, the ice-blue globes held no compassion. In a blink the snake folded back on itself and vanished from the branch. A green flash from a further bush marked its retreat into the forest.

One by one, Zane relaxed tight muscles. "Is it dangerous?"

"I don't know. It's met me here before. It always goes away. I think it's from the forest, sent to see who's here." She shook the bag. "Let's move. Darkness comes fast under the trees. The water isn't far."

‡‡

Sitting on the horse blanket, they feasted on rabbit meat and sipped spring water while an oval moon threaded itself through branches and clouds. The breeze brushing Zane's cheek carried a hint of sweetness from nearby honeysuckle. He listened to the forest night sounds and tried not to think of green snakes and great paw prints. He studied the sky, a few light specks near to the moon and many further away. He looked sideways at the woman sitting cross-legged and silent beside him. He couldn't tell if her eyes were closed. He said, "Staying here overnight in the open, will we be safe?"

She waited to answer, then said, "As safe as anywhere, I guess. Safer than some places." She whistled the same four notes she had before and Aeon came out of the trees. He walked to them through the grass and across the broken concrete. From the ground, Zane turned his face up to a giant horse standing above him at the mat's edge, wide hooves inches from his hands. "We're safe." Tawna said. She lay back and closed her eyes.

Zane woke hours later. Aeon had moved several feet away and was standing with head down. *I wonder if Aeon sleeps.* He looked again at the stars and listened to the continuous background mutter of a living forest. Beside him Tawna slept on her back, breath deep and slow. She had released her hair and her face was framed by a bronze halo. *When her face relaxes she changes from warrior to woman.* The breeze lifted strands of hair and some now lay across her face. *Would she sleep better if I brushed it away?* He bent over her. With a start he realized that her eyes were open, looking into his.

Her voice was soft. "Are you going to kiss me?"

"I think so."

Her eyes closed. "Okay, but that's all."

As before, she poked her foot into his back at sunrise. "Get up. Let's go home."

"I'm headed to Orlando. That's where I was told to go. A man said he heard that it's magical." He smiled. "At least I'll be away from Texas and can make a new life."

She had lifted a sack of game. Now, she lowered it to the concrete and stood looking at him, silent.

Zane shifted his feet. "What?"

She shook her head, then turned away and gathered her hair into a copper colored ponytail. "Let's load Aeon. We're going to find blueberries."

For the next five miles they rode through the ancient and ghostly scars of a past urban civilization. Mixed with forest detritus and vines and roots, the earth was a compost of soil with chunks of asphalt. Orderly rows of concrete pads constructed by long-ago settlers had been overcome by time. Oak, hawthorn, elm and other trees, with the help of indomitable ivy, hid gentle mounds of gray gravel streaked red with iron oxide. Occasional pillars of concrete and stone rose above the forest floor. All were blanketed by vines, their myriad roots methodically finding and forcing apart every crevice. Zane said, "I wonder what this was like when there were people here. Where did they go?"

Tawna shrugged. "There's no way to know." She slowed Aeon, looked around, and guided him off the path and through low shrubbery. Soon the forest opened to a meadow and bushes of ripening berries. She said, "Breakfast." Then she said, "And lunch."

Hour upon hour, Aeon's leg muscles moved in a repeating rhythm, carrying Zane and Tawna faster than they could have walked even unburdened by bags of dressed game. From Aeon's back they watched the sun climb to its zenith in the sky and then slide downwards on the opposite side. By mid-afternoon the forest thinned. Later the path widened. There were hoof prints, damaged plants and other evidence of use. Once they avoided meeting four horsemen carrying rifles by pausing behind a shrubbery screen and watching the hunters ride by.

The sun was low but had not yet colored the sky when Aeon halted and Tawna jumped to the ground. She said, "Everybody off. This is as far as Aeon goes. Let's get this load off his back." When the bags of game were on the ground and hidden by brush, Zane watched Tawna and Aeon walk back on the trail. Tawna rubbed Aeon's neck and scratched the white streak on his forehead while speaking softly. Then stepping back she straightened to her almost six-foot height, standing with feet apart as if fastened to the ground. For a moment horse and human regarded each other, then the horse turned. As he moved away Tawna patted his side, then slapped him twice on the rump. Zane watched as Aeon moved into the trees. When he blinked, Aeon was gone. They were alone on the trail, standing in the forest's shadows.

"Come." Tawna grabbed his arm and in twenty feet they were out of the trees and at the edge of a grass filled meadow that swept downward and around a lake, then climbed to disappear over a far ridge of hills. To Zane's left, about half a mile away, he saw a farmhouse and barn. Beyond, other farms were marked by split-rail fences. In the distance there were the log poles of a stockade. The lake, down hill from where he stood, was a half mile across with meadow, farms and a stockade on its other side.

They waded through knee-high grass, avoiding thistles with saucer-sized pink flowers shielded by hostile thorns. When they approached the house the meadow grass became a lawn with a curving flagstone walk. Pink azaleas edged the front porch where a man in a rocker watched their approach. Tawna waived. "Hi Dad. I'm home." As they came closer Zane saw that the man was not as old as he seemed. *He's frail,* Zane thought. *He looks ill.*

Shaking his head, the man said, "Tawna, I've seen you bring all sorts of creatures out of that forest, but never one like this." He lifted a trembling hand which Zane took and held for a moment.

"Dad, this is Zane." She started to say more, then paused. "If you see Uncle Bill tell him I've borrowed two horses." She pulled Zane's arm, guiding him away from the porch and toward the barn. They saddled two horses, then rode back to the forest's edge where the bags had been stashed. These they tied to the saddles. As they rode out of the trees, three men came riding towards them. Tawna said, "They're from across the lake. Hold the rifle loose but ready. Don't point it at anyone. I'll talk." She directed her horse along the tree line towards the approaching riders.

The two groups halted several feet apart. One of the men glanced at the bags. "Been robbing farms again, eh, Tawna? There's no game like that in these woods." Her eyes held steady. She didn't reply. The man nodded towards Zane. "I see you've got an armed guard. No need for that. Around here we're all friends." Zane looked into unblinking pale blue eyes. Curiosity or hate?

Tawna flicked her reins and her horse stepped forward. "You're looking well, Mike."

The other touched his hat. "You be careful, young lady." Then the groups moved past each other.

Tawna pointed ahead once the three men had passed. "We're going to the stockade. There's a cold cave there for storing meat." She glanced at Zane. "What about those guys? Did Mike remind you of anything?"

Zane's thoughts flashed back to the evening before, to the forest leaves, a green branch, eyes of blue ice.

Tawna studied his face, then said, "Which do you think is the most dangerous?" She spurred her horse before he replied.

There were four of them at the dinner table eating fried rabbit, mashed potatoes, gravy, early green beans, and jalapeño peppers. Uncle Bill forked his potato, then munched on a slice of pepper. He laughed at Zane's grimace then nodded at his wife. "Bertha and I are Tawna's back-up parents."

"Much more than that, Uncle Bill."

"Well, anyway, her mom left us years ago and her dad . . ."

A voice came from the next room. "Go ahead and say it, Bill. Her dad is dying of gut cancer."

Tawna left the table and went into the darkened room.

Bill pointed his fork at the open front door. "That forest out there, it's just a forest. Trees and all that stuff. Many crazy stories about the place. You know, dangerous beasts, mysterious happenings, that sort of thing. Travelers stay close to the path and hunters, they don't go far into the woods. Folks say there's nothing there to hunt."

Bill slid another piece of rabbit onto his plate. "But nobody told Tawna. Her first steps were toward the trees. Over the years I've talked myself hoarse telling her not to go there, but even as a kid she sneaked in, sometimes at night. Scared Bertha and me to death. Sometimes I wonder . . ." He chewed thoughtfully. "You know, in a certain way she's different, maybe special. Tawna's in her early twenties, about like you I suppose. When she goes into the forest she lights up in a special way and the forest responds to that. Most folks don't see it, but I can feel her glow for hours after she comes out. Another thing—wherever she is, she may not be the one you notice at first, but she's the one in charge. The farmers here didn't elect her to any special job but folks trust her. They follow what she says." He paused. "The community across the lake that wants everything we've got—they can't figure her out. That makes them nervous. They leave us alone."

Tawna appeared behind him and put her hands on his shoulders. "Stop talking about me, Uncle Bill. You're overloading Zane with gossip."

Laying his napkin on the table, Zane pushed his chair back and stood. "Bill, is there someone in the community who would let me borrow or buy or trade for a horse? I'm heading for Orlando. I was told it used to be a kingdom, or something. I'm going there to find land, a place where I can redo my life."

Eyes on Zane, Bill reached behind his back and grabbed Tawna's hand. He pulled her around. "Did you know this?"

She stood silent, avoiding his eyes.

He shook her arm. "Tawna, you have to tell him."

She looked down at the table. Red-gold hair fell forward, obscuring her face. Her voice was a whisper. "Zane, parents tell bedtime stories about Orlando. That's all it is. The place where it might once have been has been underwater for over a century." She shook loose from her uncle's grip and ran out of the cabin.

The men's eyes met. "Go get her, son, or you'll be counting a lifetime of empty days." Bill pointed to the door. "It's dark now but you'll do okay. Turn left, beyond the barn, maybe a quarter mile. You'll feel the higher ground. It's her favorite place."

He saw a shadow on a log bench. He came slow and sat beside her. The moon was still down and the Milky Way divided the speckled blackness. After a time he said, "It's okay that you didn't tell me."

She said, "I was scared that if you found out you would go away, back to Tampa Bay, to your boat, to somewhere else to find the new life you're looking for. I want you to stay."

He fingered her hand. "Tawna, if you'll have me, I'll stay forever. I could never find a better place than right here for a new life."

"Look, Zane." She put her hand on his arm. "Look at the forest, the trees in starlight, and down the hill the lake rippling so gently, and beyond that the hills rolling to the horizon." She turned to look in his face, tears streaking her cheeks, and said, "It's so beautiful."

Born Again

by G. Kay Bishop

PADRAIG O'FLAHERTY WAS A FINE-LOOKING MAN: a big, broad-shouldered, hearty-laughing sort of man; the kind that makes for good company—nay, the best! If you like good drink, good wenching and just grand fiddling that is, the best that ever was nor ever will be. And oh! How the man could sing! Wrench the heart out of a toadstool, he would, with that silver spanner of a tongue.

But he was a wandering man, too: one that would not, could not, should not be tied down. For the restlessness was in his bones and made him itchy all over when he staid still too long.

He came into town—one dull, dry, hot, wasted, stuck-in-the-dust little town—like the breath of Spring: the kind of Spring that has forever vanished from the face of the Earth. He might have been a mirage, shimmering out of the blue air and taking Earthly body only from the red silt floating in the haze of desert heat. For red of hair and red-faced, toting a red fiddle and a ready smile, was Padraig this day. He livened up the street just by looking at it.

Few looked back at him. It was mid-day and most folks were inside, napping until the cool of the day came on and the evening plowing might be done by the light of the moon, under the downward gaze of stars. It was the way of these little half-deserted places he knew.

A stroke of luck for him, to be sure. There was no sign of such a lonesome spot on Old Reliable, his drone-made map. The rains must have shifted more than the railroad or even the Army knew. Fields, right enough. Oats he reckoned, and barley—maybe they'll be making good brew. Pipe irrigated, for certain. Green were the fields anent the red cliffs. Might be a piece of old, drowned Erin's earth, broke off, still bleeding, and set down in this drear dry corner of the world.

Except for the complete radio silence. That was a bit of a bother. His directional scanner, makeshift as it might be, was trusty. Good as anything made of spit, shingle, and chicken fencing could be. He glanced back at his pack straps to make sure none of the wires and tangle of it was poking out. Some of these out-of-the-way places were rabidly antitek. It wouldn't do to have a run-in with any of that lot. Ah! A church, of sorts. Sadly wind-battered, but of sound fabric. Sanctuary for the likes of himself. Bless the Lady for it.

At the well, a priest sat in the shade of a high-peaked cone that looked much like a witch's hat. He smiled benignantly at a strangely subdued and somewhat sickly set of children. They blubbered at the lip, or had protruding eyes and tongues. Weird, deformed heads and limbs, idiots, retards, every kind of hideous bastard you could think of. Sweat-streaked, caked with dust. All as naked as they were born and twice as ugly. Repulsive, really. Capering round his skirts like a flock of goats, of which there were far too many for Padraig's liking in the pastures already.

Padraig started. The goats all turned their heads at once to look at him with their yellow, strangely slitted eyes. He had always felt a twinge of dread around goats: especially big singletons, or large herds. "Superstitious," said his priest. "You must have been butted as a child and never got over the fear." But Padraig knew better. He went right on crossing himself when he caught a goat looking steadily at him. He did it now, shuddering as if an icy wind had struck his broad back.

"Ye're a good Catholic then," the priest called out to him, smiling welcome.

"That I am, Father, and I'll bless you for a sip from that well, please God."

"A sip you shall have, then. Here, Lucky-boy! You and Lucy come work the well for our guest."

Two of the least disabled children hastened forward willingly to obey. With unstinted energy they set themselves bodily against the winch and raised the water. It was a game and toy to them, one usually forbidden them. They beamed on the recipient and would have done it all again though they were clearly at the last gasp of their frail strength to lift the full bucket just the once.

"I see y've got yerself a feisty flock there. Yon pullets fightin' above their weight. The hens as brassy as the cocks, eh?"

"Ye'ere not far wrong there, Mister . . . ?"

"Call me Padraig. And how shall I be naming you, when I'm asking for me last rites, as this heat chokes me to me death and lays me on the green?"

"Krysimmereski." He laughed as Padraig struggled to grasp and pronounce the tangled Polish syllables. "Never mind. Just call me Father K. Everyone else does. Come along children," he added. "Recess is over. We have a guest to feed."

Arm in arm, the two men followed the aberrant children off to the side of the huge, barnlike adobe cathedral, down two, down three, down four flights of stairs, around the corner of the church and then plunged into the pure darkness of a man-made cave built onto the back.

So dark, it was like sudden blindness and made Padraig think of Paul's conversion on the road to Damascus. Unlike Paul's, this blindness soon wore off of its own accord as a faint light filtered down from high above, through tiny slits in the thick walls, baffled and flanged and angled against the wind.

The children, with the ease of long familiarity, shuffled and hobbled on ahead down the long, narrow passage that led eventually to a flight of shallow stairs. Up the stairs they clambered, each in their own awkward way, while Father K latched the dust door behind them and adjusted the wool-baffled louvres on either side to admit more of the dry, sun-baked air. He and Padraig then took the stairs in their long strides and came up with the flock when the stairs gave way to a gently graded ramp.

Just past the steps, Father K turned back to lower a tightly woven half-panel of bamboo attached by a hinge to the ceiling of the passage. Ducking under this, he also latched together two overlapping cloth panels of loosely woven goat hair. They filtered the steady inflow of hot air. Pinging with a slight hiss against this Dutch-door dust-baffle, particles of sand and dust piled up at the base of the top step, staining the dun stone red. Father K. swept his own and his guest's feet with a handy whisk broom.

The ramp, now relatively clear of sandy grit, topped a slight rise and terminated in a room tiled from top to bottom, floored by simple geometric patterns of mosaic. Father K flipped a switch on a tank raised far above the reach of curious little fingers, and another on a hose leading down therefrom. He hosed down the squealing flock, who revelled in their meager shower and sat down in the gathering puddles on the floor, splashing like happy puppies. He turned the hose on himself next, soaking his robes to a dripping state, and offered a similar spray down to his guest. Padraig, nothing loathe for a free wash, accepted with gratitude for the cooling effect as well as the clean.

The outside air whooshed up the interior channel, whistled through the tiny loopholes situated high up in the passageway wall, into the main body of the cathedral. There were no openings to the outside in the passage, all light was filtered in from the interior of the church. Once inside the cavernous church, the streaming air rose up, up into the squat chimney of the steeple, exiting at its pinnacle where a solar-powered fan whirred with a low-voiced, steady, workaday hum. The breeze, cooled by the shade, passing over their wet clothes was most gratifying and their garments were soon dry as ever.

Now that the uniform clothing of dust was off them, the children seemed even more naked and vulnerable than before. They looked peeled, raw, stripped for a whipping. The growing light from a clerestory high above revealed their many blotches and patches of discolored skin. Now they were even more unpleasant to look at. Padraig avoided looking at them as much as possible, by attending most courteously to his host.

Together, they topped up the reservoir of the church's swamp cooler. Draped gracefully over a piercework frame next to the north wall was a vast sheet of thinnest muslin. At its foot lay a long, shallow, carved stone tray. At each end of the tray, huge double-glazed ceramic cisterns bulged out from the wall. They might have been fired on site; shiny marks of scorched earth and velvety black streaks of soot ran higher than a man's reach up the wall. Padraig trod the twin-treadle bar to work the pump, while Father K handled the bamboo pipe that directed the outflow into the tray.

A meal was prepared by Father K's own hands, for there were no women to perform the task. Padraig supposed they all went home to serve their men the noon meal. It was just so in many of the towns he had lived in. He hoped to meet the ones who were unattached, in any case, so he regretted not the lost opportunity. There would be other occasions to smarm and charm a batch of old biddies. He was a fine man, Mr. O'Flahtery, and well-accustomed to good living all around.

The meal was simple but ample, consisting of barley-oat bread—heavy to chew, but filling—and sour, goatsmilk curds, flavored with onion, garlic, salt, hot peppers and a bit of barley sugar. There was no ale but a tart drink of cactus-flavored vinegar shrub stood in the place of wine and did well enough to unparch a thirsty man's throat.

As good a meal as ever eaten by Irish kings. Maybe better. The bread had a rich, nutty taste that meant it was freshly made. Probably hand-ground flour, too. Some kind of drought tolerant variety. It yielded up an amazing flavor. Padraig made no remarks on the subject, though, beyond common thanks. He did not wish to give anyone the impression that he had been subsisting on K-and-R.

Army rations were dry and tasteless enough, but the mush-mess supplied by the railroads to their articled working men was a punishment in itself. Uneatable except by those who were literally starving. Which most of his fellows were. Himself being the exception: yes, exceptional in every way.

He had persuaded the gangbosses that he needed to be on night shift on account of his milk-white complexion. 'Twould kill him for sure, and that was not right to kill a man for hitchin' a rail ride.

And they had allowed it, knowing he could tell the priest if they refused. The Church was powerful in those parts; they dared not risk a shutdown under religious freedom laws.

Yellow devils, he thought, remembering the dispassionate, cool gaze and pale ivory faces of the Chinese overseers who bossed his work crew. All white men, by rights, though browned almost black by the sun. Big white men like himself being watched by those inky, slanted eyes. But he had pulled warm Irish wool over those eyes, right enough!

Once he was on nights, he made a habit of slipping off a trifle early to entertain the dear, duped lady who fetched him drink and brought him better food. It was indulged; most of the men did the same. She even paid his bond, meaning to wed. He pledged himself to the rail as a free man, signed the papers with a flourish and spent the signing-up bonus to spread a grand glorious, memorable feast for the men on his wedding day. And spiked the drink with vision-rye. The ergot-laced tipple gave fairy visions to all and sundry. At his insistence—for it was bad luck, else, not to toast a man at his wedding—even the managers partook. The merest sip, but it was enough to disable pursuit for a day or so.

From there, it was easy steps. He kissed his dreaming, dead-drunk bride and lit out for the East and civilization. For once, he did not wait to claim his paternal rights.

None of the crew were chained, nor even riffed. RFID chips, after all, cost good money, and the desert was prison enough. By God, he was glad to be shut of them. Let them curse him all round; he was free of them all.

Doubtless they supposed him dead. He would have been, too, barring the drone map. He had kindly liberated it from the Army just about the same time as himself. In these parts of the world, lacking knowledge of local water holes, a man was three days from death in any direction. The directional radio-scope too; the railmen had not missed it until it was too late. With it, he easily eluded his fellow townsmen's half-hearted pursuit. They were stupid enough to use radio among themselves, as they scattered in search of him. The scope also helped him keep clear of the more populous villages until the fuss had died down. His backpack well stuffed with the widow-woman's food, cactus in plenty and avoidance of the more obvious water holes, he stayed out long past the patience of pursuit.

The local Indios, asked to track down the offender, had laughed themselves sick over the story and declined to offer their assistance. He had heard them discussing it on the wire—they said it would be impious to interfere with a manifestation of CoyGod. Though he knew it was all heathen nonsense, Padraig felt a strange surge of pride. He was become a figure of legend, entered into the company of Cuchulain and other heroes. He'd be remembered for his exploits. Up the Irish and discomfit the foe!

Never remiss when it came to his manners, Padraig offered as host-gift a plug of excellent hashish, which Father K declined on his own account but accepted for the children.

"Some of them have pains that nothing else can ease. I thank you in the name of Our Lady."

A nap was in order after eating. Father K gathered the children into the shadiest, coolest corner and began telling them a nap-time story. Something about monsters that live in the Big City and eat little children for breakfast, which they received with trusting delight in their own safety. Padraig doubted that most of them understood a word of it, the lubby eejits. He lay himself down in a dark, quiet cell far from the children's corner and was soon fast asleep.

When he woke, it was evening, with the last rays of the sun fading from the rafters before his sleep-dusted eyes. People were trickling up the aisles, moving slowly, as people do in summer and in the country. Nothing of the quick march of the cities that Padraig preferred.

But time enough to talk of the city when the girls came out to blossom like dusky roses in the night. He had a mind to take a whirl with one or two of the lasses whom he saw laying planks across the tall backs of several adjacent pews, and settling them firmly into notches neatly carved for the purpose. Evidently, these were meant to serve as makeshift tables upon which the smiling girls and buxom women were draping thickly embroidered, color-rich cloths and setting out signs of plenty: a bright, tempting array of covered dishes and platters. Pork and beans. Miner's lettuce. Tomato-cheese stew. Savoury aromas drifted over to him as he stood up to arrange his tumbled dress and hair. Must look one's best when about to meet the ladies, yes?

Father K, too, was bustling about like one of the women in his long skirts, settling his odd charges into their assigned places, supplying them with food, cleaning their messy mouths and fingers. He kept busy enough! Poor man. Padraig felt all and more than all the luxury of his liberty of life and limb. He was glad to be on his own lay and to have escaped the lash and the labor draft alike. That last job on the railroad was not easy to flee. But he did it. Bless the ladies, Padraig thought, who love. Especially the ones who love too well. She had paid his bond, he knew. But he would never be going back.

It appeared that this was not going to be a church service at all. Padraig was prepared to make all the motions of a devout and humble working man, for that went over well with most women, even the ones cocooned in burkas. Many were the veils he had lifted in his day. His spirits and other parts lifted at the thought. He composed the one and subdued the other. Steady, me lad. Don't spook the game.

His cassock now stained and beslubbered with the detritus of his labors among the little ones he had suffered not only to come unto him, but to wipe themselves all the hell over him, Father K finally had enough leisure to bring forward and introduce his guest. He explained just what Padraig had told him with that simple faith in the spoken word that made so many people such rich sources of profit. All about having been discharged from his last job, the horse dead of a rattlesnake bite, his wage papers lost in a sandstorm during the desert crossing, the whole elaborately embroidered ten yards. Just enough to awaken feminine pity, not enough to make himself appear like a sucker, chump or weakling.

"So, in honor of our guest's patron Saint, we will dispense with the usual services and have a Stranger Greet instead. That means a story and song contest," he explained, turning to Padraig with a smile, "along with our usual love feast."

A shrill little voice came from one of Father K's special flock. Everyone smiled at the little fellow who stood like a rooster upon the pew bellowing his tuneless verse:

> *Who sings the best shall gaily pass*
> *The fairest night with the fairest lass!*

What luck! Padraig thought, to win some lady so lightly and at so little cost. For he divined that else, a hard spell of plowing or spudding would be asked of one so able-bodied as himself, and he had a mind to offer as small a down payment on his next hire purchase as he might. He had plenty of stories to tell in his turn and already felt himself to be in fine fettle vis-a-vis the voice. That vinegar tipple was just the ticket, truly it was.

The feast ensued, and then the folk arranged themselves in a way that was familiar to Padraig, from many a contest and county fair. The young men who were to compete were foremost, or as one might say, innermost of the circle. Next came the young ladies, and very fetching they looked, each guarded by her own father or older cousins and uncles and older men in general. Last and outermost, least regarded, sat the middle aged and old women, their fingers ever busy, spinning, knitting and what-all with needles flashing and clacking; meanwhile, their tongues running likewise in a continuous murmur like an everlastingly talk-talk-talking stream. Many's the mouth full of aimless chatter he had stopped with a kiss. Not that he would want to with those dried up specimens. Plenty of juicier lips in the second row, oh yes!

Well, the singing was bound to be better than Padraig expected. Even the old priest was astoundingly good for his age. Voice cracked a bit. Must have been a wonder in his youth. But Padraig was convinced he could better them all with his strong, manly tenor, liquid tones, and perfect-pitched pipes. He made himself ready to be called on next, as he supposed he would be, guest of honor and all that.

But Father K prevented him with a gentle hand, saying, "Here, it is our custom to call upon the stranger last. Each man who wishes to compete sings or tells a tale for the ladies to give judgment upon. Age hath its privilege. I must go to bed soon, and rest beside these little ones. So we will have my telling next. Do not be put off. No discourtesy is meant. When I have done, you too shall be at liberty to sing. And to tell us your tale. We have no doubt of your power to charm us all."

With that, Father K settled himself into a comfortable lean-back on his chair, and thus began: "Once upon a time, not too long and not too short ago, but just the right amount of time, there lived a poor, sad, and sorry sumphole of a family. The mother was mean-mouthed and whining; the aunt was prodigal with other people's savings and thrifty with her own. The daughter earned luxury by being light on her legs and easeful on her back, but she was stingy withal and as hard-hearted as they come until she died of the pox and her pimp stole all her jewels and finery. The father was feckless when he was sober and a brute when he was drunk. The eldest brother took after his father and ran with the mob for most of his short but inglorious life. The second brother was as light with his fingers as his sister was with her legs, and he too enjoyed the fruits of his delicate labors—playing the horses, the cards, and the tables to his heart's content until he welched on a bet with a bigger man and wound up the rest of his days treading the long belts at the Mill.

"But unto this sour, sad, sorry, slumphock of a family there was born the merriest, liveliest, luckiest and loveliest slip of a lad. He was not good at begging, for he laughed and spoiled the gambit. He was not good at purse-lifting, for he was clubfooted and could not outrun the marks. When he was little, he jockeyed a while, but he would not take bribes for he loved most of all the running free on the great splendid horses and the joy of giving his all. Besides, he soon grew too big and heavy for owners to hire when smaller men abounded who were not averse to padding their pockets and nobbling their own mounts.

"'Simpleton,' his father called him, slighting him with that name for his repeated failures to line the coffers of his dear Dadda's household with so much as a thin layer of silver, never mind good ready gold. But still, he was a likely, lively, lovely lad and he loved the girls and they loved him. When he sang to them they melted into his arms like cold butter on hot toast.

"Well, the time came when he of an age to wed, and since he was so well set up and handsome, his father had no trouble lining up a good match for him with a wealthy lass, but not the best looker in the bunch. But Simpleton, for all his easy ways, was not to be boxed up like a bunny rabbit fed on greens and carrots. He had a mind to wander and a happy way with him. He told his bride-to-be he must make some money to buy her a present worthy of her beauty and went away before the wedding. But he had his way with her that very night and left her pregnant, while sighing and swearing that he would return. She, in turn, sighed and swore to her angry father that her bridegroom was an honorable man, and barred him from going after Simpleton the lad.

"Two years later, Simpleton did return, leading an old, smelly, and hideous donkey, which was all he had to offer his bride. He made out that he was a simpleton indeed who had been tricked out of a fortune and told that this was a magic donkey. His bride was so enraged that she would have nothing more to do with him. The father was forced by town law to pay Simpleton some small amount of money in lieu of giving him part custody of his own child.

"In truth, he had been living off other women's charity, wooing them and bedding them and fathering children on them. And when he declared that he could not wed for he was an engaged man, then he demanded money that was due to him by law for planting the seed, just as a man might be paid for sowing a field and not being allowed to harvest the crop. And many a place paid him with money just to be rid of him and others paid him with blows, when they could. But he was a big man and no coward. So he gave near as many blows as he got and left well satisfied for having had the best of the ladies and also besting the men. He had only come home with the donkey in one of those sparse spells between bouts of baby bounty, hoping to secure yet another wad of cash.

"Now that he was disengaged, he must come up with another way to slip the bonds of matrimony and secure the blessings of patri-money, for this carefree life suited him very well. He grew ever less apt to trade honest toil for his keep and more like to spend time in the tavern fiddling for joy. If he did any real man's work it was just enough to blind fond feminine eyes, and by such short bouts of fakery win the hearts of the fair. It was ever hard work to simulate the goodness of man that was never in him, and easy to fall back on the ways he learned in childhood.

"Here, his voice stood him in good stead, for it was a lovely one that told of love in winning ways. Yet, no sooner had he won a woman than he turned his wrath upon her and drove her away. Though he was not a slave to drink, he made out that he was and escaped punishment time and time again by pretended penitence. Only those few, unforgiving hamlets where he was put to work in the fields in chains did he shun, never to go back and demand more money. After a while he began to prey upon younger and younger women and grew ever crueller in his methods of putting them off. He wandered down many a road and slept in many a haystack, but all this was meat and drink to a man like him.

"Well, at long last, after many pleasant meals and merry parties gained in this fashion, Simpleton found his pockets empty again. So he took to the road, as before, and as before won his way into the heart of a simple girl. But this time, he was in the hands of Our Lady and she guided him to a better way of life. In the first place, his new young wife was as meek and mild as any woman can be and not be choked like a chicken and et for dinner. She would not rise to his taunts and she accepted his blows and wept not, but served him as well and as lovingly as ever. He grew ever more peevish the more patience she shewed. At last, the raging need to wander made him so mad that he took up his own crippled child and dashed it to death before her very eyes.

"Well, that was the end of his wandering days. Into a prisoning cage he went, there to fan himself by the heels while the people came from far and wide to decide his fate. They were a long time deciding, for many and ingenious were the ways people had devised for him to suffer and die.

"But the fairest of all was his wife, who transformed herself before the Assembly and revealed Herself to be Our Lady in mortal frame. And She spoke wisely unto them, saying, 'The greatest punishment you can give is also the greatest blessing you can bestow.' And then she disappeared. But the people understood well her will.

"So, the good people of that far away place offered him a choice of penances: either he was to die by hanging for his crime, and the world be mercifully quit of him, or he was to take instruction in the Church and make amends for his grievous faults by caring for these innocents and unfortunates who abound in such numbers nowadays, watching over them, feeding them, cleaning up after them, and tending them in their illnesses, until such time as they died or he did. So, with a heavy heart and resentful mind, he chose to live and to serve life.

"In time—not too long and not too short, but at just the right time—these, the poorest and most needy of charges from this town and those from miles around, became not just the objects of his care, but the very light of his life. He loved them as he had never loved anyone in his life before. And the Love that surpasses all others—the Love of his born-again Lady—came to him as well.

"Now, I know that this story is true, because this Simpleton was none other than me. Yes, I who stand before you, offended Our Lady by murthering my own child. But My Lady hath redeemed me and made me to understand the justice, the joy, and the holiness of Her Way. And, oh, Blessed! How glad I am that I chose to give myself to Her!"

Now, Padraig O'Flaherty was a big, burly, two-fisted fellow with plenty of sport in him and fear of no man, give him a fair fight. But Father K, in his youth, might have been just such another, though now so old, so stooped, so mild. As he stood there, in full moonlight, exalted, with arms upraised in a fever of holy joy, it was as if Padraig saw him clearly for the first time. For the first time since Padraig came into town, he noticed that the skirts the priest wore were subtly different—not the cut of the Catholic garb he knew, but of some other sect. A resemblance that was doubtless intended to deceive.

> His heart stood still, as a wintry chill
> ran thrill through his muscle and bone;
> And the blood in his veins whispered icier strains
> of the pains he must soon bear alone.

Cautiously, Padraig raised his eyes beyond the calm, smiling countenance of the aged priest, to the rapt faces of a band of brothers: tall, strong, remarkably beautiful, black-haired young men, each one his equal in height, with strong, well-muscled, wrestlers' bodies. Past them to the ring of serene, balding soft-featured older men, each with his own lovely, long-haired daughter sheltered in his plump, soft arms, till at last he saw the all-enclosing circle of old women, the ones who were well past breeding. He looked long and deep into their gleaming, black, all-too-knowing eyes: and what he saw there fair took his man's breath away.

The story ended. Their heads all turned towards him. He stood, stepped forward and bowed to his hosts. An easy, unstrained, *practiced* smile lit Padraig's face.

"Well, Father, there comes a time in the life of a man when he knows he's bested, and that time is at hand for me. I've never heard a voice so clear and sweet as your own. I admit it without a trace of shame. I've no doubt some of these splendid fellows I see before me have voices sweeter and finer still. And I've no wish to join in competition with the likes of them. You've all got the better of me. I'll be moving along then, and God bless."

"No, my son, that you shall not. We must have you stay with us for a least a fortnight. Mother Kybele, She who is born again to rule the Earth, advised us aforetime of your coming. She greatly desires to instruct you in the Truth of Her ways."

Well, that made the matter plain enough. Many lives had been lost trying to convert those bitches from Hell to the good ways of God and Man. They fought like ten devils apiece. Their virgins suicided or strangled their own get if held captive. Poisoned their righteous husbands, Mormon, Christian or Muslim. Their men—yes, and their no-men and half men—fought to the death. The old women might be captured but they made treacherous slaves, so dangerous it was better to slay them at once. Under the truce, they were allowed to live unmolested, so long as they sent out no missionaries to spread their hateful gospel of birth control.

What bog-rotten luck for him to have fallen in with this lot! He had been so hopeful, so sure that the radio silence meant safety for him. But it only meant the bourn of no return, for cross it, and you were all theirs, by law. Sanctuary! But not for him.

He was a strong man, Padraig was. But they were many, and poor Padraig, he was alone. Pity the wanderer, ye hard-hearted citizens! For his fate comes upon him, and not a dog hath he to make him 'ware. Gaze deep in the eyes of strangers, lads, and watch for the signs of the Goat!

'Twas not that Padraig submitted to his dire fate without a struggle nor a whimper. Had his drink not been drugged, sure, he would have given them the fight of their lives. As it was, though, Padraig O'Flaherty would hereafter live by the lilt of his fiddle alone, for he would go forth and father no more.

‡‡

From the start of formal negotiations, it was clear who had the upper hand. Long before he was released on his own recognizance, Padraig was relieved of all that might be construed as contraband. That sweet relic of a drone-made 'lectronic map vanished without a trace. Likewise the radio-scope on long-lease from the M, N, and O: it too left no trail behind it. Neither Vacaville nor Vavaville would ever see either of them again. Whoever had the benefit of them henceforth it would not be himself.

The rougher part of the business transaction came down to this: life on their terms or death. It was made clear to him that he had come hither, of his own free will, to seek sanctuary and to repent. Otherwise, he was obviously bound to be a spy: for the Catholics, abetted by the Army and the Railroads, a sneaking violator of the truce, hence subject to summary execution.

Barring conspiracy, there was no other way in which he could have found them. The price of their silence about his whereabouts was his about theirs.

Alas! There are parts of this world in which it is just not safe for a lone man to wander. Curse the Trickster God who led him into this one. It was an old, *old*-time religion that had revived traditional gender roles. Roles of a sort a man did not like to think would ever apply to him. Castrato singers and eunuchs in the harem and so forth. Padraig had never been more surprised in his life than when Father K's robe parted frontally and revealed to the beaming moon his naked body, sexless as an angel.

Well, hell's own garter: a man cannot plan for every stray chance in life. His spring of luck had just dried to a murky mudhole, that's all. In the desert, a man must drink waters he would spurn in the city.

In the end, he accepted their terms, signing a document to the effect that the "treatment" performed on him was by his informed, unforced consent, in accord with his desire to repent of his sins.

That this was a bald lie did not seem to trouble his captors. No eagle trapped by a confederation of mice could have been more indignant. The injustice of it was what galled him most. He'd done not a blessed thing to this lot, not so much as touched one of their women. Hell, he'd not even got a good look at them! How they knew so blasted much about his past career he could not say. It was damned inconvenient, though. And eerie. Witchy. Those old women would have been burned in his birthplace.

Faugh! Come what may. Best head for the city where his deformity would go unremarked. Or even be praised! By those stone-hearted, flint-eyed, gold-clutching city cunts. Yes, in law, it was his own choice, a choice made in bitterness, for the alternatives offered him were worse. To live as a half man, free to piss standing and still roam, was sweeter to him than death outright or joining the Order with full caponization. Freedom was worth the purchase, even at the cost of forever holding his tongue about what had been done to him.

What good to complain? He dare not lay charges in court, Lord! For how many charges by rustic females lay primed and pointed at him? IMDs, Impudent Matrimonial Devices, easily tripped by the lightest touch of a moon-drunk toe! Not to mention sweat-debts owed to the railroad men.

No more lights o'love for him in the sweet, sultry, summery towns around. Henceforth, his high, fluid, silvery voice would win him no more wooings nor line his pockets with good gold.

The priests and mullahs standing guard over every luscious little watering hole would never believe he was not a willing convert to Kybele, nay, out on his evangelist novitiate thereof. Truce or no, he knew they were still out there, the faithless swine. Everyone knew it. Some of those ball-less bastards were brave and bold as any real man. Coercion, no contract, they claimed, and preached their godless tripe to women's ears by the dark of the moon, when the bloodfall was upon them and they were taboo to natural men.

No, no, Padraig; don't push yer luck. Best keep yer britches on and yer singing off. Stick to the fiddle, me boyo, and God damn all women here and hereafter.

CODA

THE RUSH TO ROBOTS
BY JOEL CARIS

IT NEVER FAILS TO AMAZE ME HOW SHORTSIGHTED AND DUMB we humans can be. A particular instance of this straight stupidity came to light recently in a news story I read[1]. The *Las Vegas Review-Journal* reported[2] in early November that an autonomous, driverless shuttle bus was involved in an accident on its first day of service. Critically, though, the news story assured us (with a small sense of triumph) that it was not the brainless bus that was at fault, but the brain-addled human at the wheel of the delivery truck that caused the minor collision.

What happened? It's simple, really: The bus's sensors detected the delivery truck backing up and stopped about twenty feet away so as to avoid direct impact with the truck. The truck, however, did not stop; failing to notice the adorably dormant bus, the truck driver continued to back up until one of the semi's wheels made impact with the visionary vehicle, denting the body of the bus but leaving its passengers unharmed.

The pictures accompanying the article are quite enjoyable. One showed that some clever—perhaps even cheeky—bystander slapped a series of bandaids along the crack in the bus's plastic body. A picture of a woman and small boy inside the bus revealed their looks of confusion, perhaps with the young child wondering what sort of special cultural insanity he had been born into. Bored-looking police officers wrote a ticket. One wonders who the ticket would have gone to if they determined the bus had been at fault.

---

[1] I know, I know: "Which of the some thousand recent stories indicating this are you speaking of?" you ask.

[1] https://www.reviewjournal.com/local/local-las-vegas/downtown/human-at-fault-in-accident-with-las-vegas-driverless-shuttle/

But it wasn't, of course, and I won't argue with that conclusion. The truck driver did indeed fail to see the bus, apparently being error-prone as humans tend to be. A representative of the city of Las Vegas helpfully noted[3] that "[h]ad the truck had the same sensing equipment that the shuttle has the accident would have been avoided." Of course, one might be inclined to note that if the shuttle had the same sensing equipment as the truck did (i.e. a human driver) the accident likely also would have been avoided, by the human driver doing the sensible and simple thing of throwing the bus into reverse and gently moving out of the way of the slow-backing truck.

A spokesman for AAA, a sponsor of the autonomous bus, perhaps gave the game away when he responded[4] to the accident by saying, "This is one of the most advanced pieces of technology on the planet, and it's just now learning how to interact with humans and human driving." One wonders if that means the most advanced technology on the planet still can't begin to touch the complexities of the human mind, or if it's so much more advanced than us that it finds the illogic of humans inscrutable. Considering that it can't figure out that perhaps reversing out of the way of a very large object slowly moving toward a collision with it is a good idea gives us an indication of which is the correct answer. That said, I still find much of the illogic of humans inscrutable, such as this obsession with autonomous vehicles. So who's really to say?

This news comes at a time when the testing of autonomous vehicles continues to expand onto city streets—though typically on flat, well-maintained, clearly marked city streets in places such as Phoenix and its suburbs, where snow is non-existent, rain is uncommon, and pedestrians and bicyclists are far less present than some other cities. And it comes as company after company promises that they're about to eliminate human drivers any day now, which is apparently something that we all are required to celebrate as the next great technological leap forward, no matter how many livelihoods it destroys.

The fact that such an incredible amount of money, energy, resources, and dreams have been poured into this utterly unnecessary rat hole of unemployment and further shredding of the tattered remnants of America's social and economic fabric is proof enough, to my mind, of just how insane we have become as a culture. The project of driverless cars is not just a wholly unnecessary one, but an actively destructive one, as well. Yes, yes, I see all the claims that this technology, if widely disbursed, will save lives on our roadways. I am not convinced, but I acknowledge that it's a possibility. That said, I'm sure we will of course all feign great shock the

---

[3] https://edgylabs.com/self-driving-bus-involved-in-accident-on-its-first-day-of-operation/

[4] https://www.bloomberg.com/news/articles/2017-11-10/vegas-fender-bender-highlights-risks-of-sharing-road-with-robots

first time one or more of these vehicles is hacked and purposely plowed into a crowd of civilians, and I'm just as sure that we will shortly thereafter shrug and say that this is just part of the price of progress, then proceed to exclaim over the closest shiny object. Granted, that may ultimately prove no more deadly than the use of non-autonomous cars to plow into groups of pedestrians, for which there is apparently no great shortage of willing drivers, and so again it's possible that this great project, if seen through to completion, might make the movement of cars less dangerous.

Of course, the movement of cars is not the only way in which people are killed in today's world. There are a good deal many other ways, and one critically important one gaining steam of late is through the elimination of work, income, and purpose. Not only has this trend become a commonplace killer in our society, but it is wiping entire communities off the map, shredding families and neighborhoods, devastating towns, and tearing down social stability. The waves of opioid-related deaths, mass shootings, and health crises of all sorts can, at least to some degree, be traced back to mass economic displacement. And disemployment is a key driver of that displacement.

Reducing road deaths, in other words, is hardly a good enough reason when there's a corollary contributrion to deaths of despair[5]. It strikes me that there is, and I would even argue that it's one of the key reasons behind the project, even if not quite in a literal sense. The core purpose of this project of driverless cars, after all, is the same as the core purpose of so many economic and technological projects of our time: to further concentrate wealth and resources. The goal—as seems to be the great goal of our entire economic system—is to disemploy as many people as possible. It is no longer desirable for people to have jobs, so far as I can tell; the desire is to put them out of work, to replace them with a less functional and more limited robot, and to save labor costs as a result. Never mind the human behind this displacement. Never mind that this impoverishes society as a whole. Never mind that this shreds entire communities. Never mind that this literally kills our citizens. Never mind that this can only further the tragedy that has become so all-encompassing in our modern society—that *is* our modern society. Never mind that every rich CEO, every tech billionaire, and every clueless politician who is feverishly pushing this endless disemployment is doing little more than hammering together the guillotine that will eventually take their heads. If we can't get to the stars, we damn well will at least get a robot car to drive us across town without the displeasure of a dirty human mucking up our day with idle chit-chat from the front seat.

These are the sort of great, grand dreams we have reduced ourselves to as a society. Fairness, equality, a decent living for everyone; human companionship and

---

5 https://www.brookings.edu/bpea-articles/mortality-and-morbidity-in-the-21st-century/

functioning communities; healthy ecological support systems, small and adequate supplies of energy, quality food to eat and clean water to drink; the joys of connection to the natural world, of good work done well, of neighborhoods and communities that thrive in a world made well together; all of these are dreams not worth pursuing. They must be subordinated to laziness, sloth, convenience above all else, concentrated wealth, vastly powerful corporations that know every detail of our lives and use every one of those details to attempt to sell us cheap and useless crap we don't need, all overlaid with the constant staring, staring, staring at back-lit screens that keep us always from recognizing the sheer hollow madness of the world around us. *That* is the great grand dream of modern society, that in such a world we may yet clamber into a plastic car strapped down with cameras and sensors and have it carry us across town without the madness of a human being in the driver's seat.

What is the appeal of this dream? Why is it that the answer to every economic question is more automation, less human labor, and greater efficiency at the expense of quality, and of good work done by human beings? Why do we caper after such a world, certain it will finally bring us the satisfaction and happiness we lost when we abandoned the idea of the necessity of good work?

I have no answer. I find it utterly confounding.

But what I can say, and with a good amount of confidence, is that the dystopian future of all-automated, all-the-time is not one that will come to pass. Yes, driverless cars are already on the road in a certain capacity today, and they will continue to pop up here and there, likely growing in popularity over the coming decade or so. But they will not reach the critical mass envisaged by their most fervent proponents. They are not economically feasible, even if they are technologically so. And even that is an open question when asked outside of the flattest, most well-maintained, most clearly marked suburbs.

And yes, the elimination of jobs via automation will continue apace, at least for awhile, as the pursuit of profit trumps all humanity, and all consideration of community and care. Yet these trend lines too will come to their inevitable end as the social, economic, and ecological costs wrought by our idiocy continue to accumulate and create ever-growing disruption. These projects are self-terminating. Their very ideological pursuits will create the chaos that will sow their own destruction.

While I consider this appropriate, I take no particular comfort in it. Comeuppance is fine, but far preferable is the turning away from bad ideas in the first place. It is a bitter comfort that comes from watching destructive people destroy themselves, for even if you don't care about their destruction, they inevitably take down many other people with them. We have already committed ourselves to ruined communities. We have already committed ourselves to a dehumanizing and murderous economy. We have already committed ourselves to the mindless destruction of much of our planet's ecological systems. We have already piled pain upon pain upon pain into this world, battering and bloodying so much of what we have touched—which is near everything—as an industrial society.

We didn't need to do any of that. The destruction was not necessary or inevitable; it was the cumulative decisions made by all of us, ricocheting through our culture and environment, feeding and metastasizing off our own corrupted actions. Watching the self-termination of those cumulative decisions in the coming decades will not be fun. It will be painful to live through, as it already is, and some, probably many, of us won't make it through.

But it's the sheer lack of necessity of all this that strikes me most. So many of the projects that have brought us to this point were and are so unnecessary and so pointless. It is perhaps why the obsession with autonomous vehicles galls me so much: it's about as blatant an example of unnecessary suffering that I can imagine. *Why* do we need to get rid of human drivers? Isn't it bad enough that we entrust so much of our lives to cars to begin with; why do we need to remove the small humanity within it that remains? What is the point? Supposedly safety—that's the only reason that makes even the slightest sense that has been proffered. Yet I am skeptical a world of autonomous vehicles would prove safer. I suspect it would end the same way that the widening of highways to fix traffic problems do: an ultimate return to the status quo, simply in a somewhat larger context. And should it not, there are still those pesky deaths of despair. There is still that greatest project of our time: the economic destruction of wide swaths of our population in favor of even greater economic excess for a much smaller percentage.

Another claim is that this will reduce overall driving, which is also a falsehood of the first order. This reminds me of the massive corporate agribusinesses assuring us that genetically modified crops are all about reducing the use of chemicals. If you think that Monsanto designed Roundup Ready crops to reduce the use of glyphosate, I have a Level 5 autonomous Tesla[6] to sell you. No, all the major car companies are not feverishly working on autonomous vehicles so that they can put themselves out of business. The entire point is to eliminate (paid) humans, increase the number of cars, and convince more (paying) people to become dependent on cars than ever before[7]. That the plan is ultimately doomed to failure is beside the point.

Some day this madness will stop. I would like to think that it's because we will come to our collective senses, or that a groundswell of opposition will rise up and

---

6 http://www.smh.com.au/business/innovation/general-motors-executive-says-elon-musks-self-driving-claims-are-full-of-crap-20171005-gyvd7n.html

7 http://www.sciencedirect.com/science/article/pii/S0967070X15300627

alter society in at least a few sane, lasting ways. The latter may yet come to pass in some limited capacity. But more likely is that the dreams will fall apart under a rising tide of unrest and chaos, of broken economics and shattered communities, of the ugly growths that inevitably come out of human pain and suffering. We still don't understand it as a society, but we live in a whole system. Our actions and decisions matter. Our pursuit of conveniences and shortcuts will only boomerang back on us. We can slap as many bandaids over the cracks in our society as we want, but it won't hide the cheap, hollow structure underneath. Eventually we may learn that lesson.

Or perhaps we'll just move on to the next shiny object, the technology du jour. I don't know what it will be then, but ten bucks says it will be some brilliant new idea to displace humans. It seems to be the only technology we can imagine these days.

Year Two is soon coming to an end!

Don't miss a single issue of Into the Ruins

Already a subscriber? Your subscription may be expiring!

Renew Today

Visit intotheruins.com/renew
or send a check for $39 made out to Figuration Press to
the address above

*Don't forget to include the name and address attached to your
current subscription and to note that your check is for a renewal.
Your subscription will be extended for four more issues.*

Subscribe Today

Visit intotheruins.com/subscribe
or send a check for $39 made out to Figuration Press to:

Figuration Press
3515 SE Clinton Street
Portland, OR 97202

*Don't forget to include your name and mailing address,
as well as which issue you would like to start with.*

Made in the USA
Columbia, SC
19 November 2017